Cutter's ISLAND

~

Cutter's ISLAND

CAESAR IN CAPTIVITY

Vincent Panella

Published in 2000 by
Academy Chicago Publishers
363 West Erie Street
Chicago, Illinois 60610

Printed in the U.S.A.

Library of Congress Cataloging-in-Publication Data

Panella, Vincent
Cutter's Island : Caesar in captivity / Vincent Panella.
p. cm.
ISBN 0-89733-484-1
1. Caesar, Julius—Fiction. 2. Captivity—Fiction. 3. Pirates—Fiction.
4. Rome—Fiction. I. Title.

PS3566.A5768 C88 2000
813'.54—dc21 00-044200

To

CASSIE,

CHRISTINA,

MARCO,

and

KATIE

ACKNOWLEDGMENTS

This novel was written with the help of research done at the University of Massachusetts library in Amherst. I am also indebted to my wife Susan Sichel and my friend David Calicchio, who read the book in draft stages and provided insight and suggestions. All of my family kept the faith, especially my in-laws, Frank and Peggy Taplin, whose unwavering confidence in my work encouraged me to continue. I also wish to thank my agent, Michael Valentino, Jr., as well as Sarah Olson and Allison Liefer, graphic designer and publicist respectively, at Academy Chicago. Special credit belongs with my publishers, Jordan and Anita Miller, who worked tirelessly to bring this book to light.

AT THE AGE OF TWENTY-FIVE HE SAILED FOR RHODES AND WAS CAPTURED BY PIRATES OFF THE ISLAND OF PHARMACUSSA. THEY KEPT HIM PRISONER FOR NEARLY FORTY DAYS, TO HIS INTENSE ANNOYANCE.

suetonius, JULIUS CAESAR

~

WE MAY PERHAPS LIKEN THE SOUL TO ONE
OF THOSE FABULOUS MONSTERS WHICH
COMBINE SEVERAL SHAPES IN ONE.

Socrates

Julius Caesar's Prologue

I was born during the civil war between Optimates and Populars, and learned to take one side while walking on the other. The Populars wanted to grant political rights to all Italians on the peninsula. Their champion was Gaius Marius, my uncle. The Optimates comprised the Roman nobility, who refused to share power. They were led by Cornelius Sulla.

When I was young and Sulla was fighting the Asian king, Mithridates, the Populars took over the city by force. At their head were Marius and my father-in-law, Cinna. These men presided over a wholesale slaughter of Optimates. But when Sulla returned home he defeated the Populars in a battle outside the city walls. Then he took revenge, and a period of worse butchery ensued.

Having the misfortune to be both Marius's nephew and Cinna's son-in-law, I was considered a Popular and marked for death by Sulla. He later pardoned me because so many influential friends argued that I was harmless. But since Sulla couldn't be trusted, I made my life away from the city, always a step ahead of his thugs and spies. When Sulla's power waned, I returned and began my political life. Poised in the senate like a cat with a twitching tail, I caught two corrupt Optimates in my paws and prosecuted them on the state's behalf. I lost both cases, but while my reputation for oratory grew, I was advised to refine my speaking skills in Rhodes, at the school of the renowned Apollonius Molon. Thus in my twenty-fifth year I took a trader bound for Greece, and fell into Cutter's hands.

Cutter taught in a different kind of school, and this is the story of how I deceived him, and through that deception came to know myself.

IN THE YEAR OF THE CONSULS

Gaius Aurelius Cotta

AND

Lucius Octavius

No wind, no sleep, and all night the rhythm-keeper's drum pounds in my ears. These oars pull so slowly that the Greek islands, those dark humps and breasts, those shade forms of gods in repose, float alongside as if ship, sea, and land are one attenuated dream. One house lamp in a darkened village, a shepherd's fire in the hills, these are tiny stars in a blacked-out world.

Curled up on my duffels and settled among the cotton bales, I peer at the spectral moon and pray for a wind. Without wind we're pirate bait, crawling along in this heavy tub, our tired oars pulling through islands whose caves and harbors provide refuge for pirate fleets that our government, weakened by civil war, has allowed to flourish.

We have no greater enemy, not Sertorius the Spanish rebel, not even King Mithridates who raids our border towns and calls the pirates his navy. Without these brigands to capture our ships, kill and ransom our citizens, lay siege to our ports and drain our treasury, Mithridates and Sertorius would be unable to pressure us from both extremes of the Republic.

With my attendants asleep below, the only others on deck are the captain, who works the tiller, and my uncle Curio, now crouching down and studying my face. No blood uncle, Curio is a guardian who came to us after a career as a Centurion. He served in Lower Gaul and affects the style, a gold torc around his neck, and a curtain of iron-colored hair worn shoulder length. His nose is dented from so many brawls that its front resembles the steps to Jupiter's temple.

Curio presses his palm to my forehead. "How are you, Lord?" He knows my fever signs, a dull eye, perspiration on my nose. Close to me now, his quick eyes move to the different points on my face as if activated by some mechanical device.

"A wind will come soon," I say.

"Even with a wind . . ." He leaves the thought and goes to the rail, holding his hand out in the air, but feeling nothing.

"I'll ask the gods for a wind," I tease. Curio belittles all talk of divine things. He claims that ten years serving in Marius's legions took all the religion out of him, but I don't believe it.

"A wind in Vulcan's asshole is what you need, because that's where we are. Pray for a fart from whatever god rules the realm of flatulence. See what you get. Meanwhile we're in a sea full of dangers and riding a dog of a ship."

Curio aims his words at the captain, an Italian named Secondini, who sets his tilling oar and comes forward to speak up at last. He's been almost silent for the two days we've been out, smiling as he works the big-bladed oar. Secondini barely sleeps, and lives on handfuls of pumpkin seeds pulled from his sheepskin pocket. He reminds us that he was the only captain willing to take us.

"This ship was what I had, and you took it, willingly."

When Curio has no answer for that, Secondini returns to his tiller. A life at sea having shrivelled him dry, he's small and wrinkled as a walnut. His full gray beard makes his face as round as a playing ball, and the ever-present smile seems fixed to the outside of his beard, like an extra set of teeth.

"You worry too much," he says to Curio.

"But with good reason."

Secondini waves him away and points to the cotton bales crowding the deck. "They never bother a trader like me. They're not interested in this kind of cargo. Any fool knows a slow ship like this has nothing worth taking. I've had them come alongside and look me over, then fly off as fast as falcons. Believe me, there's fatter pickings in these lanes than an old Italian with a ship stuffed with cotton. These bastards want gold coin, or rich men to ransom, like the master over there."

He gestures toward me when saying this, then spits a mouthful of pumpkin seeds over the side, pausing for a moment to watch them.

"Men like myself," he continues, coming back to the tiller, "or those few below pulling on oars, we're not worth much. We're even too old for the slave market. The slavers want boys and young men, especially rich ones."

"What about all the shipping lost at sea?" says Curio aggressively. "What about the sailors washed ashore and slit from belly to butt because they swallowed their coins or shoved them up inside their bodies? For all the pirates know, you could be playing the same game."

"For gold, yes. For gold they'd take us. That's why your master there needs to hide below at first sight of another ship. One look at his cloak and boots and we're finished. But cotton bales? They're too hard to handle."

Secondini now sets the tiller and goes to the rail, where he leans over to study the water. Below decks the beat of the drum ceases, and a mate's voice cries out that the men need a rest. Secondini, his elbows on the rail, answers affirmatively in slurred Italian.

Then he turns and says, "The tide will carry us." He points to the black shape of a nearby island to show us that the ship is moving in relation to it.

"As fast as we can row," he says, going back to the tiller and looking at Curio for vindication.

"At least he knows something," says Curio, reluctantly. His restlessness not allowing him to sleep, he stations himself at the bow. I sink into a half-sleep, then wake with the ship's surge. The oarsmen are back, and the sky perceptibly lighter with the tint of dawn. And in this way, under power of tide and oar, we creep into the house of daylight. The sun's great eye peers over the horizon, and for some time its rounded edge is clear, and dyed with subdued fire. But moments later Apollo's car bears the great star aloft so that the sea mirrors its image and we're momentarily blinded by a shower of white fire.

Such is the skill of these pirates to use nature's advantage that they choose this moment for an attack. Two distinct fireballs shot from the sun quickly become two black ships riding on a sudden breeze. They appear off our bow and converge head on, light, pitch-coated craft with red seeing-eyes painted on their hulls and swelling sails emblazoned with images of rams' heads. Fast dipping oars pull the galleys over the water with a hissing sound, and the men on board call to us in a language resembling one long, guttural word.

Secondini cries to me, "Get down!" as he raises the sail while Curio swings the tiller to turn us around. An oarsman appears on deck, sees the pirates, shouts out the word "Cilicians!"—and the panic below is instantaneous. The remaining oarsmen jump from their benches, erupt onto the deck, and dive into the cold water despite Secondini's pleas. "Don't try to escape!" he cries. "Don't anger them!" One of the galleys gives chase, the second rams us and pulls back, waiting to see if we sink.

When we don't—because Secondini removed the ballast to increase our speed—they sweep alongside and drop an assault ramp to hold us fast. Now a swarm of motley-dressed men charges across the ramp in double file, then stops at mid-point. Something changes their minds. It's Curio, waiting at our end, hefting a sword and buckler hastily pulled from our trunk.

"Who's first?" he cries. "Who's first for the dead man's float?"

"Uncle! Uncle!" I try to call him down while Secondini, worried about his crew, leans over the rail pleading for them to come back.

"Get below!" cries Curio. "Stay out of sight!"

"What do you hope to accomplish?" I cry, while the pirates, amused by Curio's plea—they've spied me already—retreat to their own deck. A few of them chuckle incredulously, or clap their hands for the show to come. Others curse at the delay of the inevitable. They pace their own deck, or fidget with the jewelry decorating their fingers, ears, and noses. The scene is static now. The sun burns so brightly we can hear it crackle. Our ship lists, and the timbers creak painfully.

Then a man screams. They've caught up with the oars men. Bowmen pick them off to the *whift whift* of darts.

Soon the victims' cries diminish as the pirates finish the job. The dead crewmen float with the tide, darts protruding from the water like the flukes of shallow-swimming fish.

"Lord!" cries Curio.

I turn, but he's no longer on the ramp. A pirate with a grossly swollen upper lip is pulling a rope attached to a pulley on the galley's mast. On the other end of the rope, and swinging over to their ship, is a drawn net containing a balled-up Curio trying to thrash free.

Now the pirates step back to let their chief through. He vaults onto the ramp and swaggers across, small and monkey-like, wearing a pitted bronze breastplate embossed with a gorgon's image. His long black hair hangs out of an old pot helmet and blows in the breeze like a stiff piece of cloth. He carries a curved sword in one hand, while the other, held out stiffly from his body, ends at a stump covered with an elaborate working of gold.

Jumping onto our deck, he pushes Secondini against the mast, pointing the sword to hold him there. Then slowly, his boots striking the deck like hammer blows, he comes directly to me, stops at some distance, looks me up and down, and bows with the flourish of a stage actor. When I fail to respond he comes closer, walking a circle around me and looking down at my boots, which are dyed red and carved with figures of lions' heads. In perfect, mocking Greek, he says, "Young man, those are beautiful boots."

I'm watching a gull swerving in from nowhere and hovering with our drift, flight feathers curled and stretched at their tips. Who is it? Some collective god of my ancestry come to give me strength? In the distance, the pirates in the other ship are hauling up the dead oarsmen with gaff hooks, and after searching for valuables, heaving the bodies overboard. They search as Curio described, working over each oarsmen like mad surgeons, ripping off clothes and cutting the bodies in those places where gold might be hidden. This sight causes my knees to twitch involuntarily, and when the deck sinks beneath me, the movement bends my knees and nearly brings me down. Aware of my reaction, the chief walks another circle around me, this time lifting my cloak with the tip of his sword to inspect my leggings, whose quality he remarks by making clucking sounds like a mother hen.

The gull is just off the rail at eye level, still hovering. It peers at me with a jerking movement of its head. Anchises? Aeneas? I focus on its little blue eye. My crafty mother, like Thetis on the sea with advice for her son? As if in a dream, I hear the chief's voice. "You're the prize," he says. "You're a year's work. You're worth ten ships, a hundred Syrian boys. A rich young man from the great city! We dream of such a haul. And where are those rich words now? Weren't you trained to speak in the face of adversity?"

When I fail again to utter a word he fills in the space with his own bragging. He's been to the great city, lived there, walked its streets, seen its mob, its pickpockets, snake charmers, games, the whores on the Via Nomentana. He's been to the place where anything can be bought, especially the politicians.

"Do you like this?" he asks, holding the golden stump up to my face. The device has been cast into the shape of a ram's head, into which are embedded two small ruby eyes. The head connects to a sleeve of fine gold plate, which ends in a leather sheath, tightly laced near his elbow.

"Pretty isn't it. Very pretty. Would you like one? Oh, still not talking. You don't talk to men of my class, your servants do that for you. And this is how I know that you're the big fish," he says. "You never condescend. Where were you swimming to? Speak up, or I'll slice off your ear for starters!"

The gull veers off and soon becomes a simple black line over the water, like the scratch of a stylus. Then it's gone.

"Speak up!"

The sword blade on my ear, as hot as violence. That part of my skin recoils. Now, words.

"Minus an ear . . ."

"What?"

". . . I'm not worth much."

"Say that again."

I repeat it.

"There!" he says, "Now the young man has words." He lifts the sword. "We'll find out what you're worth. Now, tell me, where were you headed?"

"The island of Rhodes."

"What for?"

"To study."

"To study? You all say that. To study what, and with whom?"

"To study Rhetoric under Apollonius Molon."

It was as if I'd told a joke, for the pirates within earshot burst out laughing, many crying out joyously, "The Master! The Master!"

The chief exclaims, "Ah, the great Molon, Master of Rhetoric! Shaper of statesmen! You clearly need his instruction. I see a failure here, a failure in your reticence to speak, something missing in your education. This Molon will set you straight. He's brought us the business too, believe me. We're thinking of setting up close to his school to capture more of his students. But you're way off course, too far north. Are you telling us the truth?"

"I'm obligated to tell you nothing," I say, looking beyond him to where Curio, released from the net, has been herded onto the pirate galley with the rest of my group, as if they were cattle. Let me be silent forever. The chief moves into my line of vision and says, "Give me everything you have, you Roman faggot!"

My annoyance visible, I give him my equite ring and some coins dug from my baggage. He stuffs these into his tunic with his good hand.

"Not enough."

"More is available," I say wearily.

He holds the ram's head up to my face. "Do you know who did this? Do you know who took my hand?" He turns the stump so the ruby eyes glint in the sun. He smiles now, with a softening look in his little bloodshot eyes.

"I suppose we did."

He raises one eyebrow, and says, "A smart one." Then he turns toward Curio. "Who's that old crab in the net?"

"My uncle."

"Your uncle's a slave, but doesn't know it. Wait here."

He strides over to Secondini, who stands against the mast and gulps for air like a fish.

"What's your name?"

"Secondini."

"I'll remember that, Secondini. I remember all the names. Why did you try to outrun us?"

"We didn't."

"Let him go," I say. "He was under my orders."

Ignoring me, he looks the captain up and down, nodding his head as if reaching a conclusion. He turns to one of his men as if to ask something, or to think. Then, in what seems like one motion, spins back around, his sword already describing an arc. With a blur and whistle, and then a dull, cracking sound, Secondini's head jumps from his body, then falls to the deck and rolls indecisively before coming to rest against a rope coil. The eyes blink rapidly, then stop. The smile worn for two days is still on his face, but in some way he's no longer smiling. He stares into the distance with an expression of outrage.

Someone cries, "Watch out!" as Secondini's still erect body, now spouting blood from its neck, takes a step before shuddering all over and collapsing to the deck where it continues to twitch.

The chief turns to me. His eyes are bloodshot, as if something inside him is constantly burning.

"What do you think of that?"

"What would you like me to think?" I reply, so quickly that he steps back, pretending to be struck. Backing away from Secondini's puddling blood, I lean over the rail and take several deep breaths of cold sea air. While doing this I look for the gull, which, having delivered my luck and spared my life, is perched on a nearby hump of volcanic rock stained with sea bird droppings. The wind ruffles its neck feathers as it turns to look at me. One blue eye with my gods behind it. This is everything I need for now. This will carry me.

They fire our ship, put us aboard the pirate galley, and take us northeast under oar and sail. In this part of Our Sea there are no islands. The ocean undulates with a latent, fearful power, and without reference points, sailing becomes hypnotic and mind-numbing. With the painfully slow passage of time a wall of clouds on the horizon becomes the Asian mainland with its vast, wooded mountains. Here we turn north and pass beneath palisades of porous gray marble which form the base for walled settlements. Outside the walls women spread gay colored clothing on bushes to dry, and naked boys throw stones at our ship—boys to whom the chief waves and calls in his own language.

At night lamps are lit, and the men bring a snack of roasted chick peas. The chief pours them into his mouth from a gourd held under one arm. When eating, he steers with the tiller between his knees and every so often gives me a burst of Cilician. When I ask him to use Greek—as he did before—he puts his hands between his legs and pretends to play with himself. I tell him he isn't funny.

After several hours we pull away from the coast and head westward, out to the open sea. Soon torch lights appear in the distance, then the outline of a small island. We sail for the lights, which burn in a tower on high ground near the shoreline. Three horn blasts announce our arrival, and rounding a hook of land we slip into a circular harbor with sheer cliffs to one side and a sand beach on the other. A few small craft are pulled up on the beach, and near them some cooking fires blaze. We drop anchor and wade ashore. The sickening smell of roasting meat nearly overcomes me.

~

The south wind brings fever. It whistles through the roof slates of my hut and swirls around my head, cursing like a petty god. Chilled and dizzy, I wrap myself in a blanket and open the door to go out. The guard warns me back inside. This is the fat-lipped one who strung up Curio. He tells me that Curio and the others are unhurt and housed in separate quarters, but he doesn't indicate where.

The only window of this hut looks out over the harbor and the open sea. Smoky gray clouds race across the sky and breakers rock the harbor. The chief and his men are using mules to haul their galleys up on the beach so the storm won't wreck them. Each ship is propped level with oars. Beyond the harbor mouth the wind flays the iron-colored sea into whitecaps. The sea foams at the mouth.

I lie back down and curl up under my blankets. There's a nauseous, persistent feeling in my stomach that I've done something to cause my own capture. I've missed an advantage, spurned a beggar, failed to see signs or recompense the gods. Pigeons, doves, snakes, the look in my horse's eye, something escaped my focus. This is why the winds betrayed me.

~

I dream of Servilia. Her voice is hoarse and conspiratorial. She whispers, “You’re different from the others. You’re starting late. You haven’t been born yet. Be patient, and all will come.”

“Patient for what?”

“For the rest of them to fall.”

“But they may never fall in time.”

“Everyone falls, sooner or later.”

“Then I will fall too, like Hector, like Achilles.”

“But not before changing the face of the earth.”

She thinks more of me than I do of myself.

They allow me one attendant, who rubs me down with fresh water and the last of our vinegar. He repeats that Curio and the others are safe, and I reassure him that no more lives will be lost. This is all bluff. When he’s done I turn over on my back. Sunlight leaks through the roof tiles, and I see Secondini’s face circled with fire.

~

I can trace my presence on this island directly to our civil war, which began when we took control of the Italian peninsula and drew armies from the new provinces. A Tribune named Gracchus proposed that we grant political rights to the new citizens. But conservatives couldn't bear extending power beyond those who claimed lineage to the original tribes which founded our city.

Rome never gained power through the force of logic. We are a city of blood, of emotion, and our vulnerability to attack has given us inordinate fears of conquest. We protrude into Our Sea like a bone to be gnawed by any dog, and our people see dogs everywhere: thus Romulus killed Remus, and the Optimates cut off Gracchus's head and threw his body into the Tiber. In my lifetime the same struggle was played out between Marius and Sulla, whose collective blood crimes only worsened the division between Optimates and Populars.

I was fourteen years old when Marius—six times consul—was brought back for a seventh term by his followers.

There was no election. He entered the city with a gang of toughs who killed his enemies on the spot. A nod of the old uncle's head meant your death. Anyone who greeted Marius and received no acknowledgment in return was taken down. Optimates were killed in their homes, which were then looted and given away.

I was buying things in the forum when Marius sent his thugs to purge his enemies from the senate. While leaving a pharmacist's shop I heard shouts further up the street. A group of senators came toward me, heading for the Temple of Diana with all the speed their pale, failing legs could manage. White muslins flying, and sucking air into their failing lungs, they cried out in panic, knowing their pursuers were stronger, faster, and bent on murder.

They flew past me. I knew all of them. Many had been guests at our house. They were venerable men long past their youth, who once served in the army but now made their way through the world with words, not arms. They were pursued by my uncle's slaves, thieves and muggers, ex-gladiators, conquered men paid well to do a politician's bidding. They overtook the old men and hacked them down like corn.

From the pharmacist's awning I watched as one of the victims fell at my feet. He was a distant cousin named Gnaeus Vibius, who always brought gifts to our house, a fruit basket, bowls and vases of blue Egyptian glass, pottery from Antioch. Vibius invariably argued with my father over Marius. Vibius was an Optimate, and supported Sulla. My father was a secret Popular, but he refused to take sides, after which Vibius would storm out of the house and throw himself into his litter so violently that his bearers nearly dropped him. Then he would visit again, always with his gifts, and the scene would repeat itself.

The chief doesn't know that I've seen my share of death, or that I learned to survive by subterfuge. Not that this inures me. I was so close to Vibius when they cut him down that the sound of the assassin's sword stuck with me, the way we store away certain odors. A swish like a gust of wind. When Secondini met his fate I was reminded of old Vibius. Neither man had the luck of the gods that day.

In the forum I knelt beside Vibius and turned him over, sweeping the street litter from his garment with the tips of my fingers. His head lifted quite easily and I thought to make him talk, but he uttered only a liquid gurgle. Below a brow furrowed with the burdens of life, his eyes were fixed in the distance, looking past me and watching his soul.

Power costs blood, or money. Our state has plenty of both, but not in the form of a fighting navy. This is why I'm here, and also why I'll eventually go free. Meanwhile, this interruption to my life must be borne, even if the smile is forced. The little game can be played because I have a premonition—perhaps from a seagull's eye—that I can take advantage.

~

They allow me to take the sun outside the hut, and this gives us a chance to look each other over. This is a rotten-toothed bunch with soiled leggings and unkempt hair flying in every direction. To them I'm just another rich boy, and they boast of having taken plenty like me, using the ransom monies to make war against our state. They don't consider themselves pirates, but "soldiers" of Mithridates, the Asian king and ally of Sertorius, who executed eighty thousand Roman colonists—including women and children—and then paid his way out of Sulla's punishment.

This island is their main base of operations, and lies a half-day's sail from the Asian mainland and its port city of Miletus. The men number less than one hundred, and their fleet consists of three small galleys and a fishing skiff used as a decoy. The mud hut settlement lies on the north end of the harbor, and my dwelling is one of twenty-odd scattered through a thin stand of pine and cypress. Central to the huts are some long tables where the pirates take their meals, or discuss strategy.

A tower at the harbor mouth overlooks the sea lanes, and there's more prey than these men can handle. Most of the ships are bound for Miletus. Often the men don't bother to answer the horn blasts from the watch. At best they'll send a man up to the tower to look over the potential target, and most of the time this is refused, especially now. They assume my ransom will be large, and laziness has set in.

They allow me books, clean parchments, and the writing table. During the day I read, write, or stand at my small window with my elbows on the sill, watching my attendants throwing a leather ball on the beach, or the pirates, who bring their sheepskins outside and sleep on the sand, stretched out in the sun like dogs.

When I try to leave the vicinity of the hut, even to walk the short distance to the water's edge, the fat-lipped guard stops me with a drawn sword. I'm confined to the space in front, and here I pace and review my instructions to Curio, who will be set free to raise not only the ransom, but whatever ships and men are required to wipe this rat's nest from the face of the earth.

These are Servilia's words: *Not before changing the face of the earth.* I repeat this like a prayer.

Fat Lip tells me the chief is called Cutter because of a lifelong mission of revenge for his severed hand. He beheads the captain of every Italian ship he takes—with the same trick sword stroke.

~

Such is the power of these men that they conduct their business under our very noses. Cutter returns from Miletus, where Curio has been taken to do his work, and where our governor resides. Cutter now calls me out of the hut. The men gather around, and Cutter tells them that he's learned about me from the money lenders—all of them from our city.

"We have here a Julian!" exclaims Cutter, walking around me and patting me down like an animal. "And he's more than a schoolboy heading for Rhodes—which I never believed. He has quite a history, this Roman. Descended from one of the original twenty-six tribes! He's a nephew of Marius, one of the world's great butchers and archenemy to Sulla, lately dead, whose butchery was equally unsurpassed. This young man is also son-in-law to the former consul, Cinna, who died as he lived—by the knife."

He backs off as if my powers repel him. The men applaud his antics and then follow suit, mocking me with salutes and shouts of *Imperator! Imperator!*

"But wait, there's more!" cries Cutter, bringing them to silence. "Back in the great city this young lad was high priest, called *Flamen Dialis*. He walked around the streets in a skull cap, bodyguards in front and behind. His job was to bless the temples. Touch him on pain of death! Of course, Lord, we won't touch you. We honor the great city's laws, even here on this island, which is ostensibly yours.

"But this isn't the end of it. We have quite the prize here. Our 'priest' then went to war at Mytilene, and was awarded the Civil Crown for bravery! Our own Mytilene, not two days north of here, destroyed and rebuilt! Of course you always rebuild! But we are privileged to have you! Do you have the actual crown in your baggage? We shall look for it!"

Now the pirates gather closer and I recoil from these unshaven, foul-smelling, damaged men, with teeth and fingers missing, and their women's jewelry. Some of them try to touch me, as if I'm a curiosity, but this too is in the spirit of mock homage and when Cutter restrains them they feign fright, and then retreat.

I turn my back and return to the hut, but their continued laughter and mockery draw me out again. They want me to play. Mimicking Cutter, I circle their little group, looking them up and down disdainfully.

"So, now you know me."

"Yes, Lord," almost in unison.

"You know what you have," I say. "Not some ordinary citizen, but a man of prominence."

"That's clear, Lord."

"Then treat me accordingly."

"At your service, Lord."

"Then gather somewhere else. Your noise disturbs my thoughts."

They bow low and depart, all except Cutter.

"Lord," he says. "It's time we spoke candidly."

"So this is the 'how much are you worth' discussion?"

"Lord, I have an idea."

"I'm sure."

"You know how this works."

"More or less."

"A young man like you, prominent, but not the most prominent."

He's chewing on something, perhaps his own gums, perhaps yesterday's food.

"I can see that you're thinking."

"Your wit is worth something too, Lord. Those close to you value it highly. Suppose you were released without a tongue?"

Every taunt will cost me. But what of that? One makes the best of every situation. And here I see . . . an investment.

"For a man of your experience this is taking too long. You must have a figure in mind."

"A figure, yes, Lord. Your life, your freedom, all your teeth, every finger and bone intact, you will live to eat, breed, and tell the tale, all for the reasonable price of ten talents."

"You must be joking. That's enough gold coin to fill half a fishing smack."

"Think of it as a market, with prices fairly set. Only last month a leather merchant from Tarentum brought that much. And he wasn't even a politician." He looks down at his golden arm, studying it. "It may shock you, I know. But I assure you, Lord, this doesn't happen to any man more than once in his life."

"Probably because he chooses death the second time."

"Slavery," he corrects.

I look down at my nails, which need trimming. "Aren't you just a little off the mark?"

"We don't bargain, Lord."

"You may not bargain, but for a man doing business in this part of the world, you've no more acumen than one of those African birds who spend all day with their heads in the sand. Ten talents for a Julian?"

"A prominent family, Lord."

"You still don't understand. I am the only Julian, married, wife with child, a career as bright as any star."

"What are you saying, Lord?"

"Why, that you're slow. Come now, a whole fishing smack is more in line with the handsome young man before you."

"Twenty talents!"

"Now you're thinking! I will instruct my man. The sooner he's released, the sooner we end this business."

~

Why do they hate us? Why, despite the logic of our laws, the skill of our engineers, the ability of our people to absorb other societies open mindedly, do men like Cutter align themselves against us? Because they see us not as a people, but a city so placed that it concentrates all the excesses of the known world.

A mule team leaves the stadium hauling a boat load of flesh. The carter's face is smeared with red and black in imitation of Charon. But while the Charon of myth ferries the dead into Hades, our Charon will haul them to a fly-blown pit filled with the refuse of our pleasure. Here one sees maggot-eaten carcasses of all kinds, bulls, bears, leopards, humans—all flesh being one. Whether man or beast, their faces express the shock of blank outrage. Like a cook's final touches, Charon's cargo of new flesh is well-sprinkled with freshly killed men stripped to their breech cloths. These were criminals exposed to the beasts, or professional fighters, their once powerful muscles gone flaccid, men gnawed, scratched, or hacked to death, all of them with bleeding fissures from claws, fangs, or daggers. Coins have been jammed into their teeth to pay our mythical carter's fee into the underworld. Once at the pit the criminals are tossed aside, but the gladiators are fished out and sold at high prices. Besides a lively trade in their extremities as good luck charms, their hair and blood are ground into powders reputed to cure impotence.

This is the background for my brief courtship with Cornelia, the young girl promised to me under a plan devised by our parents. I marry her, and Cinna appoints me Flamen Dialis, the high priest of the city. The first ligature between the families of Marius and Cinna.

"Marry her," says my mother. "The priesthood will protect you from the fighting when Sulla gets back. Your uncle and his son will lose anyway. They're not our blood. The old one is dying, the younger a hothead and not half the general."

Cornelia walks with me near the stadium, but Charon's boat of flesh having appeared and repelled both of us, we head for the Tiber, there to discuss the prospect of our marriage. The arrangement attracts me, and so does she. Cornelia's simplicity exemplifies a virtue too long out of fashion. She wears plain sandals, and no jewelry except tiny earrings and a plain gold bracelet. Fresh daisies have been woven into her long hair.

We find a bench on the river bank far from the route of Charon's boat. The crowd in the arena roars and stomps its feet, a signal that another gladiator is down.

"All civilized people should hate these games," she says.

"This is why we love them," I say.

"Your sarcasm doesn't negate the truth of it."

"You can't get rid of the mob."

"Yes you can. Send them home."

"But they have no home. Many are immigrants from other countries, here for opportunities that don't exist. Some are farmers from the provinces whose land was taken away and awarded to retired soldiers."

"Then get rid of your soldiers."

"We wouldn't exist."

"Yes we would, as before, a small city-nation, with our ideals preserved."

"And how many times have we been invaded since our beginnings? Ask your father."

A sudden roar from the arena saves her from responding. The crowd chants, "He's had it! He's had it!" Then we hear a collective expression of awe, a giant breath drawn in. Within moments a trumpet peals and the crowd cheers in approval.

"Can the old ideals replace the satisfaction you hear expressed?"

With a small handkerchief, Cornelia wipes the light blue cosmetic from her eyes. "I'm not a city girl. They should do away with cities, and I don't think we've been 'chosen' as a people to do anything but live together. When my father saw how tall I grew he tried to train me with the javelin, but I bent the tip around and broke the shaft. I hate this place and all its killing. I hate the crowds and the thieves and the prostitutes with their armor of cheap, brass jewelry. I hate the circus and the narrow streets and the foreigners with their pet snakes. I like our farm in Praeneste. I like cattle and sheep and wool and wheat. I like to fish and ride horses. I like being alone with the wind in grown-up fields. That's who I am."

"You're made for a family."

"And you?"

I have no answer except that I'm made for everything

and anything, a thought better kept to myself. A barge on the river momentarily distracts me. Its deck is stacked with ebony logs, and the Romans and Africans on board are making animated conversation.

"You'd like to be there," she says, indicating the barge. "You'd like to be a man of the world."

"I'm going to be." Looking at her now, at the blue trace around her eyes—probably the first cosmetic she's ever used, no doubt applied by a calculating mother. But centered on those light smears of blue are two clear eyes, of a lighter blue, and as clear as the eyes of a prescient bird.

"And what does that mean, 'I'm going to be'?"

"With respect to us?"

"Yes, with respect to our family, if there's to be one." She says that defensively, and then turns her eyes to me. This is a naked challenge, and she waits for me to reciprocate, all the while gripping the sides of the bench until the veins in her hands bulge out. Her gesture is so strong and open that I need to resist the urge to kneel down and clasp her knees, to kiss those strong veins on the backs of her hands. For a moment the pressure rises to my throat then plunges down to the center of my body. She's looking at the river. More barges are coming up, many loaded with grain. Thinking that I'm unwilling to respond, she whispers derisively, "There's more food for your mob."

"We need to decide," I say.

The hairs on her long, muscular arms glow in the afternoon sun. She takes a deep breath, and I can see why her father would give her a javelin, for she has an athlete's body, tall, and strong. She fixes on the next barge coming upriver, whose oarsmen pull to the beat of the rhythm-keeper's kettle drum.

"But you'll betray me," she says. "I know your reputation."

"Based on rumor."

"I have a choice," she says. "I could refuse, and probably get away with it."

"Do you want to refuse?"

"I think you know what I want."

"But I want you to tell me. I want the words."

"You'll get them," she says, holding out her hand. "When you get everything else."

"You're saucy too."

"I can be."

Holding hands, we enter the stadium. The air is both sweet and heavy, redolent of blood and overripe fruit. A gauze canopy pulled over the grandstands creates an intimate atmosphere. The intermission show is on. Down in the arena two novice gladiators battle with wooden swords while a squad of wrestlers fights a free-for-all. The crowd stamps its feet for the real show.

Cinna sits under an awning with his back to the arena, talking and laughing with his aides. His curly hair hides the laurel crown which he wears slightly forward.

We present ourselves and he takes both our hands and smiles with his top row of teeth. The effect is an unexpected sincerity, even an innocence.

"Now tell me, what have you two been doing?"

"Keeping away from these disgusting games," says Cornelia, in a voice loud enough to turn heads. But Cinna's belly-shaking laughter eases the moment. His large bulk gives a first impression of strength gone soft, yet there's a calculation to his pleasantry, as if he'd spent his life putting people at ease.

"Let's have your report, young ones. Can you get along with each other?"

To my surprise Cornelia clasps my hand and holds it up. Cinna takes both our hands in his.

"You won't be sorry," he says, "Either one of you."

~

Cutter returns from another Miletus trip. Now he comes into the hut, and waves his finger as if scolding a little boy. "We know even more now, Lord. Your adventures with King Nicomedes in Bythinia? Is this true?"

"Is what true?"

"This!" He waves a finger in a sign of shame. "What kind of behavior is that for a soldier of the great city? And when we found you, so far north of Rhodes, were you perhaps revisiting the old king?"

"Nicomedes is dead."

"Ah, yes!" He comes up close. He's so short that the balding crown of his head is even with my chest. Oily, individual hairs poke out from his sun-scorched scalp. He paces in front of my desk now, twisting one finger into his beard. His wandering eye takes in my surroundings, the books and parchments, the neatly folded clothing, the orderly arrangements of cosmetics and medicines, a copper tub for my bath which I demanded they unload from the trader before they fired it.

"I sense a frailty here, Lord. You've seen battle at the Mytilene siege, yes, but we don't know the conditions. Often the wealthy don't receive hard duty. Such awards like the civic crown can be . . . arranged, let's say. And these books and papers, these writings! And your fits and fevers! Your money lenders told me about those too. They say you're prone to fevers, and may even have the falling sickness, the sacred disease! We can't have you die before the money arrives. And if you have a fit? An episode? This would bring us bad luck. Are you comfortable, Lord? Do you have what you need?"

"Not yet."

"What's missing?"

"Justice."

"I don't understand, Lord. This is a simple agreement."

"My money for my life, I know. But that's not justice."

"So young, so young," he clucks. "Are you going to seek justice when this is done?"

"Why not?"

"Punish us? Capture us?"

He leans over the table, washing me in his breath of rotten meat and fermented wine. The heel of his good hand smudges the ink on one of my papers and I stare at the hand until he pulls it away.

"We have our law."

"Your law!" he whispers incredulously.

"You know our law."

He tries to fix me with a stern, penetrating look, but his little black eyes begin to move, side to side, up and down, as if their musculature has been disconnected. Then he smiles.

"Do you think you're special? There are tens of thousands like you, born into the assumption of privilege. You say what you've been trained to say, not what you mean."

"But you're thinking now, aren't you?"

"I'm thinking that I know your law, yes."

"Then you know the penalty."

"I'm familiar with the penalty, as you see it."

"For piracy."

"We're not pirates, Lord. We constitute the Navy of King Mithridates, whose lands you've taken by force."

"The butcher king has ceded Asia."

"Forget all that, and think of this: there are two parts to any law, what is written, and what can be enforced. Stick to your medicines, young man, and to your books and papers. You'll live longer."

~

I close my eyes and bring up Servilia. She is my medicine, my uncorrupt city. She is this beating heart, and she somehow rationalizes the collective din of the city, the hammers and cart wheels and shod hoofs, the sly fishmongers, the snake charmer's flute, the mix of voices in Latin, Gallic, coarse Numidian, musical Greek, Cilician, Syrian, image-sounds like the soft beating of drums. Servilia enters me the way vapors from the underworld enter the body of a priestess, through every pore and orifice.

I travel to Servilia's in a litter borne by four strong men, with six more armed with clubs to protect me front and rear. They bear me through the narrow, twisted lanes, through the blue smoke of cooking meat, through the odors of old fish, vinegar, and boiling spices.

I part the curtain of my litter and look out. Thieves lurk in the porticoes. In the open windows whores are pretending to masturbate. Idlers gather on every street corner, looking for an opportunity. These are lean, unshaven men, the mob we feed and entertain. Generations ago they were good men, farmers, soldiers, even skilled tradesmen. But they were displaced, their land taken, their trades rendered useless by cheap goods from our new territories. These idlers are victims of a confused, corrupt state.

From the streets of the Aventine Hill I look down on torch-lit barges plowing the Tiber, bringing goods from every corner of the known world: cotton, glass, mountains of grain, giant amphorae full of spices, lions and leopards in bamboo cages, oranges from North Africa, giant prawns from the Bay of Neapolis, iron bars from Mediolanum. The world feeds us through the blood line of this river. Up here the din of trade is dampened, like soft, rhythmic music. The sound is Servilia's face, for she embodies all I see. The sound is her cunning tongue in my ear, tickling in its whisper: *Not before you change the face of the earth.*

She steps into the light. A smile flickers. Her lips are as thin as knives. Is this widow old enough to be my mother? She'll never tell me her age. Her husband Brutus, a Popular who raised an army against his enemies, was defeated and executed—at Pompey's command. All this is behind her eyes, the wisdom of pain and the anger of revenge behind eyes the color of rust, like the cliffs of Cutter's island, eyes hardened with purpose, which look into me, through me, and measure me against her husband.

She says, "Sulla's back in Italy, with his army," then turns away.

I follow her into a dark space and she stops, turns, and fits herself into me as if this is already a habit.

"What are you going to do?" she asks.

Is she mine so quickly? Is she protecting me so readily? We touch along the length of our bodies and my arms suddenly feel as if they have nothing to do.

"Why should I do anything?"

"Because Cinna is your father-in-law and Marius your uncle."

"They expect nothing from me."

"Sulla doesn't think that way. Do you think this arranged priesthood will save you?"

"I don't care what he thinks," I say, my arms now around her waist, pulling her in. She fits even closer.

"You will care."

Stroking her arms, the back of her neck, one finger along the knife edge of her lips. She bites it gently.

"Do you like that? Do you like to be bitten?"

"What do you think?"

"You don't know what you're doing. You're young and eager, that's all. No, you're more than that. You're special, if you survive. If you listen to me."

~

So I wait, sitting on Cutter's beach and working my heels into the sand as if I could propel myself into the air and out of the world. The sky brightens, but the sun is somewhere behind it all, feeble and obscure. My power changes with it. Five thousand gold coins would sink that smack, and contemplating this, I'm feverish. Curio has taken my letter to the governor demanding that he pay the ransom. For failure to protect its citizens, the state should bear the cost. The chance for that is slim, thus the following:

—Letter to Crassus: I greet the city's greatest property owner. It will please you to learn, O Moneybags, O Landlord to Ten Thousand, that I have been taken by a wonderful band of pirates. They call themselves soldiers of Sertorius, and hold me on an island somewhere off Miletus. Their leader puts on quite a show, which I can detail later, if you're willing to pay for the telling. Meanwhile, if this letter reaches you through my man, please siphon some of that rent money in my direction. After all, if I were to die, you'd lose even more. This story when done will earn your undying envy. Your friend and debtor. . . .

I lie down in the hut, wrapping the blanket around my face to shut out Secondini's face and the cries of the oarsmen. Time and Money, Crime and Retribution. I'll be tested soon, and Crassus will envy me. I repeat this until sleep comes.

They burn or sink the ships they capture, but on occasion, like hunters, they return with game over their shoulders. This time they're towing a Cretan trireme with the oars on its starboard side broken off and dangling loose. They must have sideswiped it. It's a fancy ship, fitted with a bronze prow piece cast into a bull's head with silver eyes and a blunted nose for ramming. It belonged to the Cilician coastal police—who should have been protecting me—and from what I can gather from the excited talk of the men, was taken when the smoke from a victim ship attracted it to a rescue it couldn't effect.

They drag it onto the beach with mules, prop it level, then examine the hull, pointing to the features of its construction. Others climb aboard and start throwing down anything of value left by the vanquished, whose only other legacy is the blood smeared on the deck and railings, which the pirates wash off with bladders of sea water.

When this work is done Cutter comes to me and bows low, showing me his balding, mottled scalp. He signals to his men that the show is about to begin.

"Lord, is everything to your liking? Has the fever gone? Do our humble accommodations suffice?"

"No, nothing suffices."

"Pardon, Lord, we're simple men."

"That's clear."

He comes closer, walking a circle around me. Then, as if advertising my talents to a circus crowd, he says to the men, "Queen Nicomedes here is coming back when this is over! He says he'll hunt us down!"

In rough unison, his men feign fright, bowing low and begging me for mercy.

"He'll punish us under his law!"

"To the last man."

His mood changes instantly. In the same way that his eyes can abruptly lose their ability to focus, he suddenly scowls and waves his finger as if I've done something childish and shameful. He points to the trireme.

"Do you see that ship? It's a sign of our power. It thought to chase us down, but we turned and fought, even though we could have outrun it. This tells you that our federation rules the sea, and rightfully."

"That question is yet to be settled."

He waves one finger as if I'm a child who spoke a naughty word. In a whisper he says, "Before taking this government ship we went to Miletus. This is where we gather our intelligence." Then he steps back for all to hear. "We speak to everyone, especially the merchants and money lenders from your city. We mention your name. And do you know what? You're well known! The good life! The bribes and politic dinners! Your wife safely in the country while you dabble in the city! The plots and plans to power! Everyone knows your history now, Lord. They even told me about that little business in Bythinia. You and King Nicomedes!

His infamous night visit to the golden room! And you tell me you were on your way to Rhodes to learn public speaking when we came across your ship heading for Mytilene and points north? No matter, anything is possible with you people, anything!"

To their laughter and Cutter's final threat—"We know more than you think!"—I return to the hut.

That night I hear drunken voices outside.

"He's in there, asleep!"

"Let's spread his legs and poke him."

"Lord! Are you there?"

"Lord, after you return, will you show us mercy?"

Fat Lip drives them off. I go outside to thank him. His name is Hytaspes, and his upper lip is notched and bulbous on one side from a sword cut. The wound has immobilized some muscle so that when he speaks, only one side of his mouth moves. He acknowledges my thanks with an exaggerated bow, then winks and touches his index finger to one earlobe—the sign for homosexual.

~

The money lenders who fill Cutter's ears with gossip constitute the second wave of our invasions. They follow the army and carry all the rumors from home. One of them is that King Nicomedes of Bithynia and I were lovers.

When the king promised his warships for the Mytilene siege, I was chosen to collect the fleet because my reputation as a "literary" officer would sit well. Nicomedes met me at the port, took me through each of his vessels, and gave me an ambassador's dinner complete with poetry recitations.

I was later shown to a spacious room with three walls of polished gold plate, and a fourth open to the air. A small, warm water fountain flowed cleverly into a marble bathtub—towels, oils, and perfumes ready to hand—and after a bath I lay in bed listening to the ships creaking in the harbor below.

Then a knock on the door, and enter Nicomedes, alone, wearing a sleeveless shirt, baggy silk trousers, and soft leather slippers embroidered in gold. He sat on the edge of my bed and pressed a long thin finger to his lips for silence.

"Trouble sleeping," he whispered, "for both of us. But you have an excuse. You're in a new place on the other side of the world, and I'm sure you miss the comforts of home."

"And why are you having trouble?" I ask, looking sternly at the position he'd assumed on my bed.

"Don't misinterpret," he said. "But don't think it strange that I'm here."

"Why shouldn't I think it strange? You're unattended, and sitting on my bed."

"What I have to say is for you only."

"A king who earlier today spoke like an expert in ballistics and naval warfare now at the edge of my bed, and this isn't strange?"

"And an officer who showed me his knowledge of warfare and poetry. We're very much alike," he said, folding his arms as if he'd gotten the better of me in an argument. He smiled with perfect white teeth, and continued.

"Not all junior officers write poetry, or if they do, feel it as deeply as you. At dinner you matched me verse for verse, Homer through Menander. The reverence for antiquity in your own poems struck my heart. You're a special young man, and I'm here because we're like-minded."

"And what does that mean?"

"Just this. You know that I was pulled one way by Mithridates, but gave my allegiance to your people instead. The warships you take tomorrow mean there's no turning back for me. I'm committed, but I won't be taken for granted. Yet I can barely tolerate the loutish government officials your city sends us. After Mytilene, I'll ask for you as an ambassador."

"Impossible. I'm not a Sullan."

"They say he's dying."

"But not his ideas."

"Your city is greater than those who rule it. Your day will come. Return here after Mytilene is taken. Come back with the fleet. We can build something between us."

Everything about him was physically distinctive. His hair was the color of polished iron, his skin like fiery ash, as if he'd walked into the world from the burning coals of a fire in the center of the earth, that part of our star which functions as its womb, that place north and beyond the Indus River.

And yet this smoky, primeval quality was balanced by an unequalled personal refinement and graciousness. Nicomedes had a way of smiling without appearing to do so. This inner smile was reflected in his eye, and in the even, slightly ironic set of his mouth. The smile was deep inside him, and meant for everyone, from the sailors in his fleet, whose bows and obeisances were constantly waved away, to the servants who set out our meal of simply cooked vegetables and meats, nuts and fruits of all kinds, and mild, tasty wines.

Nicomedes' hands rested on the hump of blanket formed by my foot. His fingers were so long and delicate that pebbles could break them, yet they grasped my foot securely, adjusting their pressure in accordance with my reaction, with the look in my eye, the set of my lips.

"You're an impressive young man," he said, stroking my foot. Then lifting the blanket to expose the same foot, he took from a nearby table a decanter of warm oil. He poured the oil into the cupped palm of one hand. The hand glided to my foot and hung above it. Its long, skeletal fingers made a shape resembling a reed boat.

Saying, "Give me the honor of relaxing those ever marching Roman feet," he rubbed the oil into his hands, one caressing the other, the dark fingers of each so long they completely encircled the other. The action of his fingers caused the warm oil to release its scent of almonds and citrus, and this no sooner enveloped me when both his hands wrapped themselves around my foot and began to milk the fatigue out of my bones, from heel to toe.

He rubbed and kneaded my right foot, and then my left, pausing every so often to put his fingers to his eyes, a sign for me to sleep. When finished, he wrapped each foot in pieces of soft cotton pulled from out of the air, then covered them with a blanket. Giving each foot a final, affectionate squeeze, and looking at me as if to say, "This is enough," he got up and left the room. I heard a rustle of silk, and glimpsed through sleepy eyes his tall, lean body topped with silvery hair, and his skin dark and red, set in the matrix of golden lamp light reflected by the walls.

Nicomedes saw me off the next morning, having me repeat my pledge to return—a promise I couldn't keep. He gave me a parting gift, which he advised me to open in privacy. It was a gold cup with inlaid figures of priapic men making love. I kept it with my baggage—and later discovered it stolen.

~

The pirates celebrate the capture of the trireme by feasting at the tables. At great fires the men roast lamb and spits of partridges while women from Miletus serve platters of bread and fruit. Amphorae of wine are dragged from the storage cave and all the men dip their stolen bowls, or have them filled by women bearing gold and silver decanters inlaid with precious stones. Soon the sounds of a flute and soft drums fill the air, persistent and rhythmic. As the wine takes hold the women dance obscenely in front of the men, who collapse from drink before they can carry out their promises.

After a while Cutter comes inside the hut pushing a woman ahead of him. "She wanted to meet the famous man," he says, removing her cloak with a flourish, as though she were a piece of furniture. The woman is small, and wears baggy silks tied below the navel.

"Look at her," he says, rubbing his hand lightly on her smoky skin, as if to show that the color won't fade. "As young as a pony, and ready to please, Lord! She wants you, Lord. Look at those eyes!"

As if on command, her painted eyelids flutter, and she keeps one hand over her mouth to hide a smile.

"A little bashful, of course. This is because she worships you, Lord, believe me. As soon as she heard about you in Miletus she wanted to be here with the handsome soldier, the poet, the young man who defied the savage Cilician pirates!"

"And what am I supposed to do with her?"

"Lord, this woman believes in love, and this is for your benefit! So many believe that shameful story about Nicomedes. Prove them wrong, Lord, prove them wrong!"

"Get out of here."

He backs out of the hut, closing the door behind him. The woman and I stare at each other by the flickering glow of the lamps. The hand still covers her mouth.

"Do you know me?"

She nods, still covering her mouth, but now beginning to suppress a giggle.

"What is it? Why are you laughing?"

She comes up close, nearly touching. Her hair is long, and curled all over. There is about her the light scent of perfume, not flowery, but redolent of the fresh, unscented oil used on babies. I take the hand from her face and she smiles with delicate, almost transparent teeth.

Music from the feast enters the room, the soft flute, the persistent drums. She sways to it, still close to me, not quite dancing, but beginning to touch me in rhythm to the music. I take her by the shoulders and stop her.

"You don't understand. I have no desire for you. It would be impossible."

"Is it because of this?" She touches her earlobe, as Hytaspes did.

Still holding her shoulders I say, "It's because of me, and him!" I gesture outside to indicate Cutter. "It's because of what I am and what he is!"

She doesn't understand, just giggles and waves her finger, as Cutter would do when admonishing me. The eyelashes flutter like butterfly wings and she pulls away from me and takes up the music fully, caressing herself in practiced motions, as if I'm no longer in the room. I put the cloak around her shoulders and steer her out the door.

The music and drinking continue until dawn, when some of the revelers launch a boat for Miletus. Their oars splash the water sloppily until the hoisted sail takes the breeze. I watch until they're hidden by the swells. Unable to sleep, I stand outside with an erection and urinate into the wind, but this doesn't relieve me. I look down at myself, pointing toward the sea, toward my freedom.

In the hut I lie down and stroke myself—almost violently—for I resent this blind demand. So here I am, full of desire. Let me offer it up to Servilia, who understands this pressure. Servilia would coo over this like a dove, flutter her feathers and attend to me properly. So I present to the world the rod of Anchises, plunging it deeply into Servilia's heart. Planets explode when I come. And then, curled up with my head on her breast, I sleep at last.

~

To create the desired impression, I'm simply myself. But Cutter thinks there's another person behind me. This was why he brought the woman, to test me.

"Did you enjoy her?"

"We did nothing."

"What?"

I'm walking on the beach, just beyond the tower. He follows on a donkey because his legs are too short to keep my pace. To avoid him, I turn inland, clambering over the rocks to a ridge, the effort bringing me there on all fours. Cutter's donkey surges past me, bobbing its head and throwing froth. He's pulled up ahead of me to block my path.

"I paid her for your pleasure."

"I never wanted her to begin with."

"Why not?"

"That should be obvious."

"I'd like to hear that you appreciate me, my friend. Look at all I've done for you."

I walk around him, moving along the ridge. Mist on the distant islands makes them seem on fire.

"You amaze me," he says, close behind me now. "Here you are, alive! I try to provide you with a little pleasure, and what do I get?"

"You're playing with me."

"How?"

This time I block his path, grasping the donkey's bridle and stopping him. The blazing sun behind him blackens his face.

"The woman was a test."

"For what? Tell me how?"

"You were playing with me. Leave me alone now."

"But I don't understand."

"You're a liar." I turn and walk away and he doesn't follow. Now I've played with him.

~

Cutter avoids me for several days, then leaves with part of his crew. They sail off in two galleys, with the fishing skiff in tow. The skiff sculls near the lanes and drags its ragged net while the galleys conceal themselves and look for a signal.

He returns with nothing, his entry into the harbor preceded by blasts from the watchman's horn. A pair of warships from Miletus are patrolling the lanes nearby, and in effect chased him home.

"We could have taken them any time," Cutter boasts, pacing in front of my hut as a way of performing for the men. "We're a federation, and you're the enemy. You!"

I don't come out. I've stopped giving him an audience when he stands outside and calls me at the top of his lungs.

He stalks off after the harangue, then comes back. One of his men carries bundles of chamomile and burdock root brought over from the mainland. But this time he stands quietly outside and announces himself. Then I let him in.

"What are you writing?" he asks, coming up to my table.

"Something you wouldn't understand."

He reads the first few lines of my poem aloud, and I see in the forced, incredulous movements of his bushy eyebrows that he's found an opportunity.

And as for Hector, before the Skaean gates
tragic destiny pinned him cold, that fatal and
irreversible verdict of the Gods which no mortal
can oppose, for it is like the tide . . .

"This is poetry? Poetry makes men cry. This makes me laugh."

"Your business is murder and theft, not art."

"There's an art to that," he says, combing his beard with the fingers of his good hand. "But I wasn't always as I appear."

"Why should I care what you were?"

"Because you're a poet, one of the privileged class, and maybe a young man of destiny—for I believe you see yourself that way. Your interest in those around you should be inherent, insatiable. And who knows, what happens to you on this island may someday find a way into your work, into your view of the world."

"How do you know it hasn't?"

"Because I know your kind. There's a presumption of privilege and superiority."

"And what is the source of that?"

He raises his eyebrows like a clown, then taps the parchment where I've written my lines.

"Lord," he says, "Maybe I'm wrong about this poetry, but maybe you're wrong about us too. We have some education here. Some of us were scribes, and some grew up in wealthy families with tutors in the Greek fashion. These men are familiar with all the great stories."

"These . . . savages?"

"They're men looking for wealth and adventure, no different from the legionaries of your great armies. Only here they have more freedom."

"To steal and murder."

"Please, Lord, these are relative questions. Why don't you recite for us down at the tables, when the men are celebrating. Maybe they can appreciate what you have to say."

"How do I know they'll understand?"

"Don't worry, Lord. We'll surprise you."

He goes down to the beach, and talks to some men working on the trireme. I hear the words, "Great Epic Poet!" and then several of them look up toward me and wave me on, clapping their hands. Soon other men join them, and they approach the hut, clamoring for a performance.

Their spokesman is a fat man named Goras, in whose little black eyes I detect a glow of sensitivity. "Young Lord," he says. "The way hungry men share bread, share with us your art. Try us, Lord. This island is isolated and untouched by well-born men. Please Lord, a few lines for thirsty souls."

~

Too cold to swim, so I imagine myself doing it. From the beach to the harbor mouth and back is about a thousand paces—one mile. I swim that twice, without rest. Stroke by stroke, I recite the Hector poem, seeing myself before the men. The poet recites and holds them spellbound. Their emotions follow the rhythms of my words.

Whilst behind him Priam's son, played by
that cunning Athena. . . .

On the day of my capture I looked over the rail of Cutter's flagship to the sandy harbor bottom. It was wrinkled like the corners of Servilia's eyes. In her sleeping room we make love by the reflection of water on the tiles. All night long we swim our lovely mile, stroke by stroke, four times, five times, even six, our breathing as regular as tide wash. At daybreak we eat a peach bursting with juice, and which, when laid open, displays delicate red veins in its white flesh.

My mind is my salvation.

~

By the glow of a charcoal heater I part Cornelia's robe. Her skin reflects the fiery light from the coals. I fondle, sample, and while describing her beauty to her I think about coming into her profound depths and there scattering sperm like a farmer broadcasting seed. She pushes me away and tells me I'm never satisfied. Later she sleeps, and I feel the vibration of a delicate snore. The sudden furrow of her brow marks a fleeting dream, while in the depths of her calmness and sleep the child is trying to form, trying to live. This is what she doesn't understand, that I am satisfied. I begin to think in satisfied ways: that I should leave the city, abandon all intrigues, get rid of my bodyguards, become a quiet senator from the provinces pruning his fruit trees and writing bucolic poetry while the Sullans rape our state.

But if I can't sleep now I wouldn't sleep then. So I lie awake and plot my next step, my next play for influence, my paths through the city, the way a pissing dog defines his perimeter. To the sound of Cornelia's innocent sleep comes the howling colloquy of dogs and wolves, and the long cry of a bear, which silences all.

By first light Cornelia is even deeper in sleep, and as the sun's eye opens, I'm off. Curio holds my horse on the far side of the stable where we can't be seen from a window. His eyes turn up to me, bright and black.

"Be careful."

"You say that every day."

"Every day that Sulla comes closer, his friends grow braver."

"What can they do?"

"Cut you into little pieces."

I mount up and look down at him. He had all his hair then, just as long, but combed straight, sleek and black. His eyes had the same lively color.

"Is that your only advice?"

He mounts his own horse, then looks toward the house. "Be careful there too. Your world is smaller than you think."

When the horses start moving I want to explode that world, break out of it. Cornelia's world belongs here. Mine belongs wherever I am. We hold the horses back at first, letting them compete, exciting them, making them strain their powerful necks. Their ears flick back for our commands. We hold back, then let loose. Mine is a high stepper, tail like a banner, fast as a dart, and the feeling of power between my legs, the wind driving tears from my eyes, and the sound, the dead, reckless, abandoned beating on the turf—this removes all trivial thoughts. There's nothing but my thunder. Beside me, Curio flattens to his horse's back, his leg muscles tight as rope knots. Now wind, thunder, and the edge of death! Now secret whispers to the gods! The horse turns one ear my way and I whisper, "Take it! Take it all!"

Curio magically falls behind.

I slit a lamb's throat and drain its blood into a silver bowl. Another priest holds the poor creature until the convulsions stop, and then my practiced dagger cuts from anus to neck, careful not to puncture a gut. Parting the rib cage I cut out heart, liver, lungs, and place these on the plate still pulsing with life. Spotless organs keep temples open.

But I have other business too, conducted from my villa on the Aventine. Borrow money from this man, flatter that one. Hire eight louts to heckle a senator as he passes the forum, settle disputes between clients. And receive. Receive men looking for work, traders seeking markets, spice and pottery distributors wanting the tax laws changed, smelters and metalsmiths needing introductions, ambitious politicians who would march against the government simply because they believe it's their turn at the trough.

In the star-filled night I stand at Servilia's atrium pool. The glow of moon and stars illuminates my shadow on the water, but not its features. Who is this gawking, overgrown thing that the palpable pressure between his legs and between his ears, like a pair of horses, hurtles him forward? Cornelia says he's just a man, and should act like a man.

Servilia's not so sure. Servilia thinks he may be a star, a brilliant orb that illumines the world. He parts Servilia's robe as he parted Cornelia's, and what does he see? Not Cornelia's virginal bush—Servilia was pregnant when they killed her husband—but the clipped and perfumed shrub of drive and ambition.

We see each other as history.

"You're thinking," she says, suddenly there by the pool, a shadow in a long white shift. So did goddesses once appear before men. But why does she think I'm special?

In her room we light the lamps. Wrinkles radiate from her eye corners and faint age lines run down her neck. But her body is smooth and firm, her breasts alert, aggressive, her nipples the color of blood.

"Don't look at me. Don't evaluate me."

"Turn around."

"No."

"Why not?"

"You make me feel vulnerable."

"I want to see the map of Italy on your back."

She turns and I trace it, from shoulders down to the coccyx, lower Gaul to Mediolanum, to Brindusium and Rhegium—all mine, not in the sense of ownership, but of spirit and idea.

She turns around and presents her front, her lips in a close-mouthed smile. I hover and look down at myself, ready to penetrate, ready to seek. We connect, lock, that perfumed shrub is the gateway to a sweet, netherworld where she clings to me desperately.

"Don't worry," I say. "Don't worry."

Apollo is just raising his whip as my litter hustles through the cool, cluttering streets—the Flamen is forbidden to ride a horse within the city walls. My curtain stays open. A metalsmith's hammer rings through the streets. Butchers are already at slaughter and animal squeals announce the city's hunger. I weave around the carts and food stalls. A garbage-eating dog eyes me. What enemy is this?

The Marians are preparing for Sulla's return. He's defeated Mithridates in Asia—for the time being—but placed our name in infamy by sacking Piraeus and burning the Acropolis at Athens. Now he's back to retake the consulship, joined by Pompey and Crassus. Weary with the burden of his own violence, Marius lies down and dies. His son, Marius the Younger, will defend the Populars outside the city walls.

Servilia says Young Marius will lose and that I should leave the city.

"This isn't your time," she says. "Leave here as soon as you can."

Her faith in me is a secret treasure.

~

The beach smells of hollow shellfish and salty weed. Snails and mollusks drift into the tide pools. A wall of haze covers the mainland, and above it Apollo whips his horses into a dead run. He's higher on the horizon now, and the blinding sphere, approaching its spring arc, finally warms me.

Like a woman being loved, I lie on the sand and take in the sun. Close my eyes and spread my arms and legs, admit the energy of gods and ancestors to the center of my being, admit my family line to Aeneas, who passed here on the way to Italy one thousand years ago.

A thousand years of tide on the stones, of dead and desiccated shellfish, a thousand years of sea swells, a thousand years when the Venus-born Trojan fought his way through the Greek line with Father Anchises on his back, and then set sail for the place whose name he didn't know, that peninsula thrust into the center of Our Sea. Above and around him the gods raged and bickered, played with his winds, wrecked his ships, knocked him down, but he always stood back up. The gods rewarded his faith and persistence. They gave him a ship, a breeze, a bladder of water, just enough, all to the rhythms of the very sea before me, all to this backdrop to life, rising and falling.

The gods, the sea, one thousand years ago when the Greeks launched their ships and flew to Troy like a flight of cormorants. It could have been yesterday.

I sit up, rubbing the dreams from my eyes. The day will come when hard life replaces these easy dreams. And this young man half-naked on the sand, chin resting on his drawn-up knees, will have to keep his word.

Three blasts from the watch and Cutter's men launch their galleys, pushing them down the beach and into the harbor, the oarsmen pulling hard even as the stragglers high-step through the surf and clamber aboard. All oars working now, Cutter's little fleet shoots through the harbor mouth, using no sails, for the day is windless, and the sea like polished bronze.

Cutter remains behind and invites me to the tower, pointing to a trader in the shipping lane, pulling its way north. It rides low in the water, as ours did. From our perch we can hear the grunts and curses of its oarsmen, who are visible through portholes in the ship's sides.

Cutter leans on the parapet, shading his eyes with his good hand. His galleys fly at the target like birds.

"Even if you catch it," I say.

"Yes?"

"You'll pay in the end."

"You and your stupid law."

"It's more than the law."

"What is it, then?"

"A way of life, a way of reason."

He turns to me with his hands still cupped over his eyes. The tower is made of hot, radiant white stones.

"How old are you?"

"Twenty-five."

"You have much to learn."

"So do you."

The trader changes direction and a second bank of oars now reaches into the water. To the rhythm-keeper's now-rapid drumming the banks of oars rise and fall. A voice cries out and the crew unfurls a great square mainsail. It begins to roll and flap before they secure its corners, then the ship creaks with the strain and its prow digs into the sea, cutting like a plow. A wind just in time! The wind god punches the sail, and the ship surges forward, outdistancing Cutter's galleys.

"This is a sign that you're going to lose. From now on you're going to lose everything."

~

Servilia knows the Sullans will kill me. She takes me into the arms room and shows me old-style curved swords, helmets trimmed with eagle feathers, ancient javelins, their heads bent and rusting, and attached to the shafts with loose wooden pegs. From the wall she takes down old circular shields with insignias of the famous legions—Larks, Horsemen, Lightning Throwers. She lifts up an antique bow strung with her grandmother's hair and explains how the women gave their hair for bowstrings when the Gauls took the city generations ago.

"Do you show me these weapons to inspire me? And to what?"

"To what you were, and what you will be."

I place the bow around her neck and pull her in. When she speaks to me that way my heart expands and presses against my throat.

I'm about to embrace her when the door opens.

"Mother?"

It's Marcus, her son, squeezing sleep out of his eyes with the backs of his hands.

"Do you want a story?" I ask.

He pulls me into his room, which contains the usual collection of toys, a leather ball, some wooden legionary weapons which all boys own, a desk with tablets, writing tools and several books.

Marcus leaps into bed and shuts his eyes. I cover him up and sit beside him.

"Tell me," he says. "Tell me now."

"If you promise to shut your eyes and go right to sleep after it."

He takes my hand. "I promise, now recite."

I begin from memory:

And as for Hector, before the Skaean gates
tragic destiny pinned him cold, that fatal and
irreversible verdict of the Gods which no mortal
can oppose, for it is like the tide. . . .

Marcus shuts his eyes during the poem, and the apprehension on his face gradually turns to sadness. His eyelids begin to flutter.

"It wasn't fair," he says when the poem is finished, as the tears come. "Hector was the braver warrior."

"Yes, but Hector didn't have the luck. Remember that."

"That's what you always say."

I put my palm to his forehead and he holds it there. "Luck means having the gods on your side, no more than that."

"And how does that happen?"

"By winning them over."

Moonlight seeps through the shutters and prints a pattern of brilliant lines on the nearby furniture. I lie down and shiver. Servilia piles on the blankets and gets in with me.

Her hand between my legs kneads me, milks me. "I don't want to lose you, but you can't stay here. You must leave the city."

"You won't lose me."

She pledges herself to me and the flow of her tears on my face tastes like sweet sea water. Yet coupled with this love is the thorn-prick of fear. My blood runs hot and cold. From the streets I hear the commands of officers, soldiers in hobnailed boots in fast march, the neigh of horses, the explosive clatter of carts. The Marians are forming. They will defend at the city gates.

This may be our last time, and Servilia holds me to it. At your service, Lady. Let me die now, let them come from behind and kill me. Let life be brief and passionate.

~

Cutter arrives at my door. He bows slightly from the waist, without his usual insulting exaggeration. I look him over, the way he did to me on the trader, up, down, and condescending. He's wearing a leather tool belt and an old tunic smeared with black pitch. He looks up with his ironic grin, and one of his little black eyes is moving around, the other fixed.

"Come," he says, beckoning with the fingers of his good hand. "I want to show you something."

"What is it?"

"The new ship. I want to show you what we're doing."

Together we walk to the beach, where the men are working on the trireme. He's about to put his good hand on mine as a gesture of friendship, but stops the gesture midway. The hand is sticky with pitch and I've already recoiled.

"We're stuck here together," he says. "And we might as well become friends."

"At least until the ransom arrives."

"At least. We should treat each other as equals."

"I think you have something else in mind."

"Which is?"

"Something you want to prove, something you'll never stop wanting to prove."

"And what is that, Lord?"

"That you're unpredictable. That I'll never outwit you."

Laughing, he leads me down to the beach where his men have put scaffolding around the trireme. They're smearing pitch over the hull, for caulking and camouflage. He explains that after the pitch has been applied, the ship will go to Miletus, where carpenters will install an assault ramp, and a small castle to house a catapult.

"With this galley I can fight or run, attack or retreat. It was a great find, Lord."

"And you'll improve it with my money. You'll use my money against my own kind."

He rolls his eyes. "Money is like rain and the sea. It rises and falls. And I'm sure you feel the same way, otherwise you wouldn't have agreed to a generous ransom."

"You know nothing about what I think."

He sighs and looks upward, as if asking the gods for patience. "You're still a boy, despite all your outward sophistication, all the stories we hear about you." He wiggles the fingers of his good hand in a sign of falling rain. "Is the source of my money any different from yours? Compared to your race what I've done is a grain of sand to all of this beach."

"How long have you been on this island?" I ask.

"Why? Do you own it? Do you own it the way you own Greece, or Sicily?"

"We own nothing. Our law unites . . ."

"Your law is rape and murder. Your law sucks people dry. Your people simply assume and take. This island, this sea, is part of Cilicia, part of Asia. Now you take it and tax it. You tax the farmers and fisherman and tradesmen. You tax each house and double it for every additional door. You're the pirate, not me."

He spits on the ram's head, shines it on his tunic, and holds it in front of my face.

"Some day I'll tell you how this happened."

"Why?"

"To give you a picture, of yourself."

With great slaughter, Sulla defeats the Marians outside the city walls. I hide at Servilia's until the battle is over, then head for the Colline Gate disguised as a tradesman. Revenge is already under way. Execution squads comb the Aventine, taking over the Marian villas—including mine—murdering any Marian supporters they find, often dragging them out of their homes and cutting them to pieces in front of their families. Many of the dead aren't Marians at all, but personal enemies of the Sullans. The victims' heads are stuck on pikes and paraded through the city, or thrown against the walls and crushed under the soldiers' boots.

The air reeks of burnt wood and fabric—furniture, curtains, pillow stuffing. Outside the gate the smell changes, to human flesh. Legionaries' bodies are stacked like logs and Sulla's men are burning them in pits as fast as slaves can supply fuel. Severed heads on javelin points line the road.

Defeated in battle, young Marius flees to Praeneste with the remnants of his army. There Sulla besieges him, catapulting his enemies' heads over the walls. This terrifies the populace, and without their support, Young Marius can't hold on. He tries to escape through the town sewer, but finding Sulla's troops guarding the exit, falls on his sword.

Sulla also publishes an enemies list, with my name on it.

~

This descendent of Venus broods on the swells while cormorants guard the rock tops, wings spread to dry their feathers. What can these black birds offer me? Either bad luck or reality. I pace on the sand, waiting, waiting, drying my own feathers. My life has been one retreat after another, either open flight or calculated absence. And if I survive the Sullans, who are still in power, should I wait my turn like any other soldier in the whorehouse of this world? Or take my luck on the tide? I could start here, on this island. If only I felt Servilia's breath in my ear.

Not before changing the face of the earth. Could this be? She's seen the signs. My severe fevers, in which I ramble on about the gods, my "sacred" fits, in which rolled muslin is forced between my teeth to prevent me from swallowing my tongue. She reads special destiny in my restlessness, my disdain for food, and the flight of doves that circles her villa when I depart all sing my name.

She sets me completely on fire.

~

After Sulla's victory we move about the countryside in a cart loaded with wine casks, one of them empty. This is my hiding place at the checkpoints.

Sulla decorates the road markers with severed heads. They're powdered with dust by now, the eyes pecked out by birds. These poor faces are a final punctuation to ideas and causes. But a face without life is not exactly lifeless, for a man's last emotion shines through an ostensible neutrality. You see at first a mask, blank and transparent. This is death's last joke. Stare at a dead man's face and you soon penetrate the mask to his emotion at the moment of death.

At one of the checkpoints an officer taps the casks and finds mine hollow. He calls me out, then shows me a cart full of bloody sacks and opens one up. The heads inside could well be melons if not for the hair, and the fetid smell. I see the blood-drained face of a young man with vacant blue eyes and a shock of golden ringlets.

"Pretty, isn't he," says the captain. "They caught him coming out of a barber stall." He ties the sack shut, then turns to me, drawing himself up.

I scratch a figure in a wax tablet and show it. He shakes his head. I scratch another, double the amount. He sniffles, rubs his hands together, looks back at his men and says, "If we were alone." I double that figure. He says to me, "My head would be in that sack if I let you go."

They bring me back to the city. Outside in the forum and under a vine arbor fittingly hung with rotting grapes, Sulla holds audience. They say he has skin like oatmeal. This is an understatement. His face is an eruption of blemishes, a ravage of inflamed, flaking and scrofulous hide. Such a face would drive anyone to murder, out of jealousy for all mankind. He looks at me with eyes like melted wax. He's already dead, already a blank-eyed statue.

"Say hello to your cousin," he says, smiling.

"What cousin?"

He points to a pedestal not twenty paces away, upon which the head of Marius the Younger has been mounted—above the following, inscribed large:

Learn to row before you try to steer.
Aristophanes

This is the great man's humor. The last time I saw Young Marius he was outside the senate with six or eight henchmen, bullying a senator. He kept his index finger in the poor man's face. He was taller than his father, more handsome, and a greater bully as well. He had spaces between his uneven teeth so you couldn't tell whether he was angry or smiling. He looks no different in death than he did in life, except, perhaps, more peaceful, and released from his father's burden.

A sword on Sulla's table holds down some parchments. He shuffles them as if looking for something.

"Why did you flee the city?"

I let him peruse me—red boots, purple cloak, hair trimmed and perfumed, every beard hair plucked so I'll never need to shave again. The process was painful, but this might amuse our blood-lusted Sulla, for he writes poetry, enjoys theater, and is open to any piggish amusement, especially with young boys.

"Why did you flee after the battle?"

"Who wouldn't?"

Saying, "I know you better than you think," he picks up the sword and points it at my groin.

"Servilia," he says, sighting along the blade and parting my cloak at penis level.

"She and her crew of politicians plead for your life. They tell me you're harmless, and barely a man. They say you have no politics and expect me to believe it."

His fingers on the sword grip are long and white, the nails scrubbed clean. If their grip tightens, I swear this pretend faggot goes for the knife in his boot. Sulla will ride in Charon's boat with me.

"Give me one reason why I shouldn't cut off that thing for which Servilia so desperately pleads."

"If you want me to beg for my life, I won't. You know who I am."

"Yes I do. You married the daughter of Cinna! This is why your name is on my list!" He slams the table with the flat of the sword, scattering inks and scrolls and tablets. "The real you hides behind all that female garb. You're the ghost of Marius—no different from your cousin over there—and you'd slice this Republic down the middle and replace its guts with liberal ideas. You'd weaken it so every stinking Italian on the peninsula would have the vote. Next would come Gauls and Spaniards and even Syrians. They wouldn't need an army to take us over."

"If I wanted to bring you down I would have left Italy to join your enemies."

"You're too cunning for that. You know I'm strong. You know I can take that one-eyed prick, Sertorius, and lying Mithridates and anybody else who comes against me!"

He lowers the sword and says, "Do you want to live?" Without waiting for an answer he hands over a parchment—a divorce decree for Cornelia.

"Get rid of her and you're pardoned."

"For what crime?"

Now he speaks with false intimacy. "Look at it this way, young man. This little thing of yours," and here he points the sword at my groin once more. "And that little thing," he taps his temple with one finger, "have gotten you confused. Keep your ambition between your legs. Restrict it there and live to be old and happy. Live until you can't get it up any more, and after that, take your pleasure from dreams and fantasies. But bring it up between your ears once more and I'll cut it off! Divorce your wife and you'll come out of this a rich man. Those numbered among my friends can buy any number of properties. You can have another villa to replace the one you lost, and for the price of a good horse. This will show you that I'm ready to make peace."

I set the decree back on the table.

"I can't do it."

"Why not?"

"You shouldn't have to ask."

"Then take your chances."

7

"You're a rich boy," says Cutter. "But what have you seen? Where have you been, to Mytilene? By the time you arrived with Nicomedes' fleet the battle was over. Is that what you did for your civic crown? Delivered a fleet to another commander? Any slave could have done it."

He looks at me with pity, then takes something from a pouch and holds it up. It's a bridle piece, cast in the shape of a scorpion.

"Gold-plated bronze," he says, "From the great Pompey's horse. Now there's a man with accomplishments to his credit."

"It could be from anyone's horse."

"Trust me, Lord. I fought against him."

"Where?"

"In Spain, at the River Sucro, as a slinger under Sertorius."

"And why did you fight for him?"

"I fought for King Mithridates, the friend of Sertorius. The two of them are squeezing you east and west right now. We may still push your guts out."

"You don't understand the march of history."

"But I know Sertorius. He can win, Lord. He can win."

"He didn't win at Sucro."

"Nobody won that day, but Pompey led a cavalry attack that sounded like the thunder of a hundred storms. He galloped on a charger covered with so much gold we were almost blinded, for the attack came early in the day and the great man was riding into the sun, as reckless as Alexander. We gave him a volley and he was hit by three stones, each strong enough to kill a bull."

"And?"

"And nothing! The first stone was mine, the smoothest in my pouch. I cried out, 'Here's for you, Pompey!' before letting fly. The stone hit him in the shoulder, and should have torn his arm off. Then two more stones struck, one denting his shield, the other his chest plate. Even above the din I heard the armor collapse. But he just kept coming, no helmet, the stones flying past his face as if gods protected him. He had a fancy stabbing spear in one hand and a round shield in the other, embossed with shining iron as only a strong man can carry. His long hair streamed behind him, flowing like music. Believe me, Lord, this was the image of a god, Achilles himself, the very sun! But then he took a dart in the leg and gave up his horse, which was torn to pieces. And such was the struggle for the great man's souvenirs that the horse was hacked to pieces and we nearly lost the battle."

"Why do you tell me this with such elaboration?"

He winks at me, as if we share some secret. "I'm not a simple man, Lord. What you see around you, the coarseness of this life, even of my past, says very little about me. I know men and their motivations."

"Do you think I envy Pompey?"

"Pompey is the man right now, until Sertorius and Mithridates put him to rest. Believe me, they will."

"And I? Who am I?"

"A man of dreams."

"And you know my dreams?"

"I know one of them. To return and punish us."

"Do you think it's a dream?"

"I think it frightens you."

"Yes, perhaps. But I'm going to do it."

~

Where am I? Sitting at the base of the tower and shading my eyes to scan the misty Asian coast, dreaming of what took place beyond that mist not very long ago. History's greatest men have trampled the mainland facing me—Croesus, Xerxes, Alexander—men whose bones are common dust, yet in whose category I count myself in dreams that only Servilia understands. *Greater than Pompey. Greater than Crassus. Even greater than Sertorius.* I need her to reaffirm my destiny, my ancient lineage, my link to the gods.

The land and sea around me is ours, every stone, every tree, every grain of sand underfoot. But not in the sense that we own it, not in the sense of property, but of security and law. And it is here, on the edge of our republic, that King Mithridates swears to the peace made with Sulla, but sends his raiding parties across our borders and uses fleets of pirate ships to attack our state. And what does our governor do? Nothing. And I? Wait, and consort with the enemy.

I don't know where I fit. Am I really a man of dreams? Am I as strong as Sertorius, who can march fifty miles a day in winter with no food and no cloak? Am I as brave as Pompey, who can ride into a hail of stones? Am I as rich as Crassus, who owns half the city? Do these men pass their days lying on the sand pulling dreams from the sun?

Pompey charges with a long spear. Stones fly past his face and clang off his armor. After the battle the soldiers hail him as *Imperator*. The cry from their ranks shakes the earth.

I never divorced Cornelia. At least that's to my credit.

Cutter's worried about the money. It's been too long since Curio was left in Miletus—on the doorstep of the governor, a Sullan who surely hopes this fop is already dead after hearing his message—that our state, by not protecting its own citizens, owes me the ransom.

So now Cutter stands in front of my table chewing his lower lip and the tuft of beard beneath it. He looks out the window toward the beach, where some of his men argue over what to do with me. The loudest voices want me gone, to the slave market in Delos.

"Do you hear that?" he asks.

"I hear a group of savages, and it's your job to control them."

"I'm not a dictator, Lord."

"Nor a leader."

He laughs. "This is why we like you, Lord."

Reminding myself that I'm lucky to have lasted this long, I close my tablet, fold my hands over my chest, and lean back in my seat.

"You know the choices and always have. Kill me outright, take me to Delos, or wait for the money. You're the chief."

"All three options are under consideration, Lord, believe me. But you bring up a sensitive point. I'm the chief, but only so long as I deliver. Those men down there . . ." and he gestures helplessly toward the beach—"are losing patience. They would like to take you over to Delos. But my argument is that only your servants have any value. And with your fevers and fits, to say nothing of your un-slavelike disposition, you'd be considered little more than a hunk of flesh, long and skinny at that. Those slavers have physicians to look men over, and they don't miss a trick."

"That's your argument? It has nothing to do with my ransom being more than you'd earn in five years of smashing up ships with those toy boats of yours?"

In response he pulls on his ear, directing it to the window, where the voices from the beach grow louder and angrier.

"There's a division here, Lord. Those of us willing to be more patient with you and with your governor, have developed a kind of affection for you. It would be hard for us to kill you, or send you to Delos, where your only value would come about if they broke your spirit, probably by maiming you in ways we all know about. We're not butchers, Lord."

"You're not?"

"Look!" he cries, "They come!" He motions me to the window, where I see Hytaspes and several others approaching.

"Who do you think they want?" he asks.

"You!"

"But that means you! Don't you understand, we're tied together. If I fall, then you fall!"

"What will they settle for?"

"I don't know."

"Call their leader in here. I see now that I'll have to do your job."

He calls in Hytaspes, who enters the hut walking like a large African monkey, slightly bent over and with his arms hanging away from his body.

Cutter says, "This one is already angry, Lord, because your man was allowed to defy us, and I let him go."

Gesturing with his fat hairy arms, Hytaspes begins to speak. Because of the defect in his lips, his voice is a low passionless monotone. He directs his words neither to Cutter nor to me, but toward the window, where the other malcontents are looking in. The gist of his speech is that the agreed ransom isn't enough. When he's done he looks at me directly, his watery black eyes beginning to shift as soon as I hold them. I turn to Cutter.

"Now I see the game."

"What game, Lord?"

"This game. It was foolish of you to set so low a figure for one so important as I am—descended from the original twenty-six tribes who claim divine lineage beyond recorded time, married to a consul's daughter, and nephew to a general who has defeated the known world's fiercest armies."

"He's right," says Cutter, stroking his beard and looking up as if he's discovered a new star. Hytaspes, only now catching the direction of my speech, begins to nod his head.

Raising my voice so those outside can hear, I say, "Let me make it easy for you, and set a figure more worthy of my station, a figure impossible to disagree with."

"Which is?" they ask, almost in unison.

"Fifty talents, more than double the original twenty. Send word to my man and he'll raise it."

"But how long do you expect us to wait?" asks Hytaspes.

"It will arrive sooner than you think, or want."

"And what does that mean?" Hytaspes puts in, as he heads for the window to confer with the others.

Cutter steps forward and winks at Hytaspes. "Until the young man takes it back."

"Takes what back?"

"The money," I say. "Every coin of the ransom money—when I return to punish you for your crimes."

Cutter nods to Hytaspes as if to humor me. "He's sworn to capture and punish us, don't you remember?"

Hytaspes smiles.

"But in the meanwhile," I say, "get out of here. I'm paying for my privacy."

Cutter bows low and backs out of the hut. This time nobody laughs.

~

Here's how Servilia tells me where I fit. I fill her mouth with more sperm than she can swallow and she rubs it on her breasts until they glisten.

"Now," she says, "lick it off." And as I lick, "Don't be frustrated, little baby. They'll make you governor of a province and give you two legions. Of course I'll be an old granny by then. You can fornicate your way around the world and I won't care, but you'll always love me, won't you?"

"I'll always love my granny."

"Then give me what you have. Give me all of it."

Making love to Servilia is like riding a horse at a dead run, and gladly plunging into the abyss, searching for the absolute bottom. I pound her like a hammer. I seek, I seek, but find no bottom. She sings in my ears like a Siren. Tears run down from her eyes. My legions march across the territory of her chest. I am . . . *Imperator*. I come swooning like a woman, then collapse and cling like a child.

Later she tells me that men take power the same way they make love.

~

Cross the island to the white-capped sea off the west beach, into the wind. A knifelike pain in my stomach makes me want to fall to the sand and curl up like a worm. Double the ransom, double! Paying money is like dying.

Further along, two great rocks jutting up from the sand offer shelter from the wind. I stand between them, hunched over. The pain in my stomach is the figure in my mind. In coin, one hundred and twenty thousand, enough to sink a boat, or raise an army. Now a sudden dizziness, and I press my hands against the rocks to hold myself up. The crash and howl of water and wind seeking me out. Let the elements force the pain from my stomach until life is only what I see and hear. I have no more thoughts.

Was I ever so weak, so alone, so without gods or divine powers? I have no more, no ancestry, no concept of honor. I'm a dead shellfish with its guts pecked out by gulls, as inert as these rocks bearded with weed and smoothed by the water's hands.

Living is like eating sand.

When my head clears I continue along the beach, pushing myself into a fast walk, fighting the thought of being nothing, disconnected, forgotten.

Washed up on the sand are Neptune's gifts, clay shards, a broken mast, a shredded sail partly buried in the sand. I pull on the sail but it won't come out. It's made of cowhide, too stiff to grip tightly. I pull harder, setting my feet, pulling until my fingers ache. Nothing. I dig around it with the mast and pull some more. The parched cowhide breaks in my hands. I heave the mast piece unto the surf and keep walking.

In gold coin—twelve thousand pieces.

~

At night Cutter staggers up with a jug of wine and calls me out. I find him sitting on the ground, his eyes rolling so they almost disappear. He puts the wine to his lips, then rejects it.

"*Non Missio*," he says, raising his jug to the sea in salute. "Do you know what that means?"

"Everyone knows what that means."

"But not what it's like."

"And you do?"

"I know what it's like to be a piece of shit."

"And I don't?"

"You just think you do."

He tries to speak again but his stomach heaves and he takes several deep breaths to stop himself from vomiting. He waves me off and goes away.

The next day we get into the skiff and I row him to the deep part of the harbor where the sand beach abruptly turns to sheer cliffs of rust colored stone. Fingers of sunlight poke into the shallow sea bottom. He sits in the stern rubbing the stump with his good hand. His eyes are steady now, and at one point they turn up to me and lock.

He tells me his real name—Vatinio—and that he spent two years in a gladiator school at Capua. *Non Missio* was their guarantee to patrons: no defeated gladiator asked for mercy.

He then dismisses the subject with a wave of his hand, and directs me past several caves at the base of the cliff. I row the skiff past these and he shows me a large cavern where the new trireme is tied up. Silver seeing-eyes have been nailed into the prow on each side, and the oar blades and woodwork are also trimmed with silver.

"With this ship," he says, "No one can stand against me."

Later he takes me to a storage room, a below-ground cave, its entrance hidden by some innocuous shrubbery. We enter a chamber as large as a villa with enough supplies for a small city. Saying, "What do you think? What do you think?" he shows me rows of amphorae filled with oil and wine, stacks of copper ingots, sword blanks, ash handles for spears and tools, and a mound of ivory tusks.

He digs into a trunk with his stump and stirs up coins and jewelry like a cook making stew. Hanging from his ram's head are snake bracelets and bulls-head chokers. With his good hand he lifts out daggers with ivory handles inlaid with precious gems, a sword belonging to Mithridates, its handle inset with a gold image of Alexander—which he kisses.

"We descend from him, all of us."

"Was he a pirate like you?" I ask.

He closes the trunk carefully and looks up, as if summoning the gods for patience. "These trinkets ripped from the extremities of your brethren had been ripped from others. In the end, all is even."

"My money too?"

"Forget about the money."

My laughter echoes in the cave.

~

The poet stands before his audience, parchments in hand. But this is no Aventine salon, no dinner given by some venerable, guests reclining on brocade couches and sipping watered wine, puckering their lips over medlar fruits. This is Cutter's island, where pirates with the presumption to call themselves the navy of Mithridates swill like hogs, stuffing meat into their mouths as if stanching wounds, gulping down Samian wine as fast as they can fill their stolen bowls.

"Sing to us, Lord!" cries Cutter. "Sing of gods and heroes."

I play to the vein of truth behind his mockery. Somewhere deep in all of these monkeys is the love of music, the love of poetry, the love of art and civilization. I can play to that. There are days to sing, and days to get even. Today, I sing.

Goras stands up to establish order.

"Quiet down! The Master is going to recite!"

A chorus of obscenity. Someone calls me "Queen Nicomedes," and Goras chases him down the beach, throwing handfuls of sand after him.

So the poet endures, still waiting for silence, his hands steady on the parchment. Goras returns, panting. I thank him and survey the divided crowd.

"The title of this will suit you. It's called 'Treachery.'"

And as for Hector, the fates pinned
him where he stood, and like an oak tree
putting down roots deep and wide, he set
himself before the Skaean gate, to prevail
or be taken down, his eyes fixed on the
dread Achilles, who stepped from his
chariot, then took a long, ashen spear from
his charioteer; hefting it, he looked for
the balance point on the shaft.

While behind Priam's son, cunning Athena
wearing the likeness of Hector's brother
Deiphobus, spoke in these strong words: "We'll
take him together, you and I, who of all your
brothers was closest, and who chooses not to run
before the blood-crazed Achilles."

And Hector the Horse Tamer, forcing the
words to join his hard-running breath, replied:
"You, brother, whose eye for women is matched by
bravery in battle, I've seen you leer over
milky Helen, and can say that spirit extends to
warfare. Of all my brothers you've always been
dearest, since as boys we fought together with wooden

weapons and held off the rest of our companions. Always we battled side by side, and now confronted by one born immortal and knowing not how the Gods have weighed our fates, with you above all I would gladly go down in death. And if Apollo helps my arm, together we will triumph."

Then Hector threw his own long spear, not knowing until too late that his brother's voice and image were an illusion, a manipulation of Athena whose breath in his ear had clouded his mind, like fog walking through a forest with steady, unrelenting step. And then the great Horse Tamer, seeing that his spear had clanged off the seven-layered bull-hide shield of Achilles, put his hand out to his brother for a second spear, and not seeing it, turned to a wisp of Olympian fog.

Thus fate sealed great Hector, as
Achilles' spear hissed like a snake, and bit!

Silence when the poem is done. Goras looks at the ground and bites the nail of his small finger. Cutter taps his stump gently and repeatedly into the palm of his hand. The rest seem unmoved. A few of the men look uncomfortably at each other. Hytaspes shrugs and holds out his palms to signify emptiness, then everyone erupts into laughter.

"What savages you are!" I cry.

"Lord," says Cutter, in a cautionary tone, "be careful."

"Come on," I say to the men. "Didn't you understand my poem?" But they aren't listening. Cutter has given them tacit permission to resume their gluttony.

"Did my poem mean anything to you?" I ask. When they ignore me, I say, "Can such ignorance exist in this part of the world, two days' sail from where it happened?"

I turn to Cutter, who shrugs and looks up into the trees.

"Every one of these men should know the story and sympathize."

"I'm sure they do, Lord. But as I tried to tell you when I first saw your poem . . . sympathy isn't what's needed." And here Cutter brings his eyes down from the trees, glances at me furtively, and settles a gaze into his wine bowl. He drinks long and deep, exhaling when the draught is finished, as though he'd found an idea.

"This business of the gods . . . is a little dated. And your treatment of Hector is perhaps too naive. Achilles was the hero. Even we know that."

"Better men than you have heard this poem, and praised it highly."

"Perhaps, Lord, but gauge the men's reaction. Many were hard put to pay attention."

"What do those brutes know about poetry?"

"Please, Lord, all men crave art. We know this. Your poem was good, and showed great facility with the Greek language."

"Is that all you can say? That's an insult!"

"You're being oversensitive, Lord. Here's the proof: with the exception of Goras here, who would love whatever you wrote, it's obvious that everyone else is unmoved. Men want more than sympathy from art. They want a model for life."

"What life? A pirate's life? A life of theft and murder?"

He motions that he wants to speak to me privately and leads me away from the tables.

"My life, yes! Do you think some Achilles hasn't held a point at my throat while I begged for life like a dog? You know what *Non Missio* means! No mercy for a fallen gladiator! So fuck Hector and whether Zeus weighed his fate on the scales and kicked Apollo's butt down the mountain and all your other effete, Greek-tutored bullshit! There is no Zeus! Hector lost, they sacked the city and that's the end. Your job as a poet is to sing about that, not to complain!"

~

A fever day. Vinegar rubs and burdock tea. Illness is like a pet dog, in and out of the home, always at the wrong time. No sleep—the world spins when I close my eyes.

Nothing from Curio, and Hytaspes still argues to sell me in Delos. One day and it's over. They'll cut off my balls and throw me in a cage with a wad of cotton between my legs. Cutter is on my side. He stresses to the men my reputation as a spendthrift. He makes fun of my poetry to show them what a fop I am, but deep down, he respects it.

The reading was an intimacy they didn't deserve.

~

Ready to move, but to where? From my writing table to the beach, where yesterday's wind and tide wipe away my footprints. This island has no record of my life. I find that liberating, and there are whole days, when, thinking of the future, I wish my stay would never end.

Cutter catches up to me on the donkey, which he has beaten into a froth.

"Lord, we have news from your man! News from Miletus!"

"Which is?"

"The ransom will be paid."

Walking faster, I say, "Then your death is near."

He plants the donkey in front of me. "Your luck is boundless! The governor will have the ransom at Miletus."

I walk around him, mocking. "Prepare for the end."

He cuts me off again. "Stop!" His eyes roll, looking for patience. "Listen to me. About the other day, Lord."

"What other day?"

"After you read the poem. Some of the men . . ."

"Yes?"

"Would like to hear more."

"They know quality after all."

"Listen to me, Lord. Whether you know it or not, this can save your life."

"My poetry?"

He leans over and puts his face so close to mine I can smell his stale breath. His little black eyes look as if they might explode from their sockets. "Will you do it?"

"Why should I if the money's coming?"

"Because we don't know when it will arrive. The men need to be distracted, like your mob at home."

"That's your job." I wave him off and continue walking.

~

Night visit. Awake to a hand on my forehead, and Curio's unshaven face nearly touching mine. This isn't a dream. The oil lamp is lit, and he's searching my face for the signs.

"Fever, Lord?"

"Very funny. How did you get here without being seen?"

"Arranged by Cutter, and I was seen, by one who'll never see again." He partly unsheathes a bloody dagger and smiles grimly.

"The great chieftain assured me there'd be no watch on the seaward beach. There was, one man."

"Who was it?"

"The fat-lipped one who caught me in the net. A sign, Lord, that there's justice in the world."

"Cutter wanted him out of the way. You were used."

"No matter. Justice isn't done yet."

"What have you been doing?"

"Hounding that asshole governor for your money."

"And?"

"A hard man to find, Lord. The honorable Marcus Juncus spends most of his time in Ephesus, where the brothels bring their service to his hotel door."

"And when does the money arrive?"

"As soon as the lenders come up with it. Consent and delivery are two different matters. Juncus is in no hurry to arrange it."

"Why not?"

"Pride, Lord. He knows you threatened Cutter."

"So?"

"Through certain contacts in Miletus, our one-handed chieftain keeps his tongue in the governor's ear, all the while filling his pocket."

"How can a governor justify that?"

"Because every so often we sweep the seas and solve the problem of these pirates. We're too weak to do that now, so why not levy a 'tax' until our state raises a fleet. Your threat to return and punish these pirates offends him, believe me."

"It will cost him money."

"Not only that, but you'd be doing his job. This will make him look ineffective back home, especially because you're so young. He told me this in so many words. Provincial governors have so many years in which to accumulate. How else can he retire with a farm in southern Italy and a villa on the Aventine?"

"So we were taken prisoner to make him rich. Our captain was killed so the governor could stuff his pockets."

"Please Lord, don't be so idealistic! Our honorable governor wasn't pleased with your generosity with the state's money either. Fifty talents is no easy sum to raise, even by a governor who wants to do it."

"I'll remember that."

"I advise you to. So how did Cutter take your threat?"

"I don't think he believes it."

"You need to practice the 'command voice,' Lord."

"In this situation? Perhaps it's better to pretend I don't mean it. Or to keep him guessing."

"You're probably right. But how do you feel?"

"About what?"

"Keeping your word."

"How would you feel?"

"Frightened, but willing."

"That's a fair assessment."

He places one hand on my shoulder, then rises to leave. "It will be a first, Lord, a first for you. You'll make your mark at home."

"I don't think about that."

"You're talking to me now. . . ."

"I'd forgotten. Then it's possible?"

"Yes, but there's work to do. Men are being recruited now."

"Good men?"

"Retired legionaries, youngsters without prospects. This part of the world is full of them, and all hungry."

"Pay them well, but for success. We'll need four good ships."

"Ships are another matter."

"The governor's coast guard?"

"Hired by him."

"Then they'll work for us. Offer the commanders enough to sway them. The money's not important. This can be done in two days."

Curio's eyes brighten. I've brought out the soldier in him.

"Patience for now," he says.

"Just remember the importance."

"Your first command, Lord." He grips my shoulder hard, then leaves. But his words remain behind, *first command, mark at home*. There was a first for Pompey when, with no authority, he recruited an army in southern Italy and presented it to Sulla, with himself at the head. A first for Crassus when he did the same. Both men were my age or younger.

I dream of many like Curio in my service, small, wily men who can march all day on flat bread and vinegar.

Now that Cutter has announced that the money is coming, everyone is more relaxed. I spend the morning throwing javelins with the men and to everyone's surprise, beat them easily. My best throw is one hundred and twenty paces. Goras massages my right shoulder before each throw, his eyes half-closed in ecstasy. He says, "You can do everything, Lord, everything." I explain how none of them have the proper throwing technique, to release the javelin at a one-third angle and follow through on the horizontal.

In the afternoon I win the foot race around the harbor and tease them during the last part, throwing back my taunts.

"You're heavy from an easy life, from too much meat and wine. You should work for a living like everyone else."

"Why should we work when you can support us?"

After the races the pirates begin a bout of eating. Whole roasted lambs are unskewered onto the table tops and ripped apart by unwashed hands. So plentiful is the meat and so poor their manners that they eat only the most tender parts, flinging the sinewy parts at the dogs. Their meat still sickens me, even though they roast it black over a hot fire. The lamb is too heavy and keeps me awake, the goat smells like its own feces. Partridge is the only meat I will taste, but these haven't arrived in time. The pirates apologize for this all around.

So I eat flat bread dipped in oil and some fresh broad beans. This is my best appetite since the capture. Tired and satisfied, I break open each bright green pod and eat the tender beans, each one an orb of energy, each one a little sun. I stare at each bean reverently before placing it in my mouth. Some of the men see this and laugh. They consider me precious and distracted. All to my advantage.

Hytaspes washes ashore on the seaward side, his throat cut. Now everyone's on edge, and this is the worst time for a messenger from Juncus. The alarm sounds and a ketch flying the governor's pennant arrives in the harbor. The messenger no sooner steps on land when the pirates, thinking he has the money, rip up the insides of his boat. Finding nothing, they strip him to the breech, tie him to a tree, and threaten to cut his heart out.

Cutter rescues the messenger and brings him to me. He's a young Syrian with a sparse beard and pushed-out teeth which prevent him from closing his mouth. This gives him the look of a simpleton.

"He's here to see if you're alive," says Cutter. "The governor doesn't trust us."

"Why should he?" I turn to the messenger. "How soon will the money come?"

"I know nothing about the money. My instructions are to find out if you're alive and well-treated."

"In accordance with his station," says Cutter, bowing low. "His every wish is fulfilled."

~

In the battle outside the Colline Gate, Pompey took the left, Crassus the right, and Sulla the center. Sulla's part of the line collapsed. Pressed hard, he pulled a small statue of Apollo from his saddle pouch and cried out, "Help me! Help me!" The Archer was with him. With their backs to the city walls, Sulla's troops were unable to retreat, and went on to a great victory.

Only louts like Cutter believe the gods are dead.

What happens to the dead? They walk in cities packed with keening souls, places of semidarkness where these multitudes of shades seek out their ancestors to compare life stories. Now Fat Lip walks in one of those cities, along with Vibius and Secondini.

I'm never alone since Hytaspes' death. I tease Cutter: those who slit his throat could have been after me—his prize. He snarls at that, and restores the guard outside my hut. He tells the men I need to be protected, then looks my way and winks. On my walks a pair of guards follows me at a distance, or Cutter himself comes along, riding sideways on the donkey.

One morning we climb a path to the cliff above the harbor. The caves are just below us, and the ram of his new trireme can be seen protruding from its berth.

"We're in this together," he says.

"And what does that mean?"

"I'm fighting for your life."

"You're fighting for my money."

"Yes, your money. But your obligation doesn't end there."

I turn my back, and continue slowly up the path, listening to the donkey's uneven step behind me and the dull report of Cutter's whip on its hide. From the cliff the glittering harbor can be seen in its entirety, as well as the tops of the trees near the settlement.

"We're in nothing together," I say, hustling along the crest and leaving him behind. At the high point I stop and wait. When he catches up I take hold of the donkey's bridle and stop him.

"We make no bargains, we form no alliances with anyone but our own."

Then I turn and continue along the crest. The sea is all around us now, an infinite sparkling sheet in which the shadows of clouds extend like continents. There's not a sail, not a bird, the view clear to the Asian mainland with its endless forests. Visible for the first time are some dark shapes resting on the water's surface, the distant northern islands. Freedom is everywhere but under my feet.

"You people!" he says, shaking his head.

"What does that mean?"

"You acknowledge nothing."

"This is why we're strong."

"And we're weak?"

"The truth?"

"Yes."

"You have no system."

"Of what?"

I speak into the air, into the sun's fire reflected there. "You have no system of origins or ethics, no potent view of man and god to hold you together. This is why you live by force and deception, why the concept of keeping one's word is foreign to you. You've been conquered and divided since time began, and always, you lost to the west. Your religion is a fragmented, inarticulate system built on the images of horned beasts. We link our divinities to the virtues of man. You're trying to say I have an obligation beyond the money. To do what?"

"To forget this incident when it's over."

"Then you take my promise seriously."

"Why shouldn't I?"

"No reason at all."

"Follow me," he says, whacking the donkey so a cloud of dust rises from its rump. We descend to a small cove protected by two walls of weed-blackened rocks reaching into the sea and defining a small beach of white sand. A deserted hut sits above the tide line. Inside we find a few tin spoons, a broken bowl, and a rusty gaff hook which Cutter picks up and examines.

"This old man was living here when we took the island. He sold us fish for several years and claimed to know the future. He predicted the weather as well as our chances for success on several missions. Often we'd find him sitting in the surf in a kind of trance, his beard soaked, the seaweed gathered between his legs like a bunch of serpents, mumbling incomprehensible repetitive sounds. He'd say he was talking to the gods.

"One day he came to deliver his catch and told me that in a vision he'd seen me drinking water from the ocean. 'What does that mean?' I asked him. He didn't answer, and disappeared after that, leaving all his belongings behind, including the skiff, his most valuable possession. The ability to endure this loss signals the potency of his vision."

We sit outside the hut and Cutter begins working the gaff into the sand, as if to dig something up.

"I believe the old man saw my death," he says, looking off into the distance. "Drinking water from the ocean could mean lying face down in the water, the way a dead man floats."

He continues working the gaff into the sand, pulling it toward him, bringing up wet stones and small bits of shell.

"Maybe he did," I say.

He looks quickly at me, then away.

"In the end, all that matters is how you live, not how you die. Life is cheap today, and luck is always on the prowl. I live to be free of you. This means I do all in my power to weaken your city, by taking its goods, money, and people. That's my life, and if I end up doing the dead-man's float, so be it."

"You must believe the ransom is worth more than the harm I'll ever do to you, otherwise you'd kill me."

"Of course. What can you do? Come after us when this is over?"

"Do I have a choice?"

"Answer your own question, Lord."

He turns to me, but I maintain the path of my gaze straight down to the placid surf. I don't see the surf from my present perspective, but from the ocean. My ships land there in the faint light, ships like death's black shades, and with a clanking of weapons the men disembark and form up on the beach. I inspect the ranks, and the hairs on my neck stiffen. All feeling runs out of my legs.

"A difficult question," I say, picking up some sand in my cupped hands and letting it fall through my fingers.

"Perhaps I can answer it. I know you as I knew so many others. A young man of moderate ambition, a nephew of Marius who barely escaped Sulla's retribution, living his life on the periphery of power. A faggot perhaps, or more likely one of those two-way types of which there are so many these days. You're well known for fancy food, tailored clothing, and poetry recitation. You also have a taste for other men's wives. This tells me something, Lord. Sulla taught you that sticking out your neck can get your head cut off. You wisely play the fop, and I'd play it for years to come if I were you. Sulla may be dead, but his generals are still in power—Pompey and Crassus. They're the bright new stars, and you know it. Believe me, I know all about you, Lord. I know the names of your wife and child, how much property you own and what it's worth. This is my business."

"And what does all this tell you. Will I return or not?"

He digs more with the gaff, and with a speculative look on his face as if trying to bring the answer up from the sand. Apparently finding none, he throws the tool aside, then runs both good and bad hands through his hair.

"If the old man were here," he muses, gesturing to the gaff hook, "he'd have the answer. But since events are uncertain, I think it best you know about me."

"Why?"

"Because wherever you go, whatever your decision, you'll understand the depth of my anger toward your people."

cutter's story

"On the docks of Miletus I grew up as a pale-skinned urchin with hollow cheeks and dark eyes. At a young age I'd learned to use those liquid eyes to exploit those who came to sample the city's pleasures. I was one of a group of wharf rats who prostituted themselves, or lured the unsuspecting to dark streets where their money or lives were taken.

"So I was a street pirate, but my idols were the sea dogs, those men with ears and noses spiked with jewelry, fingers sheathed with gold and precious stones. Their purple-and-gold-trimmed galleys defied your state most openly, and operated with the approval of provincial governors by exploiting their greed.

"I signed up, and they took me on. But without the streets and alleys of the city to protect me, without my fellow wharf rats, I was vulnerable, and learned what uses there were for a young boy at sea. At first I was passed around like common property, but then a fierce Egyptian took me for his lover. And for the satisfaction of his persistent desires I was rewarded with gold, and protected from abuses by the others. So the pirate life became another reality, like a dream. And it was easy work. Our victims rarely fought back, and between my regular pay and my lover's gifts, I soon had a sack of gold in my duffel.

"But pirates, no matter how much of the sea they dominate, never rule for very long, and the time came when your people took control. Fleets of warships hunted us systematically, and one day we were set upon by four quadremes in the Euboean Channel. Our flagship was rammed and sunk, and all its men drowned or killed in the water by dart men. My own smaller galley was boarded and towed to the nearest land.

"While ready-cut timbers were unloaded for crosses, the Roman commander addressed us. He was a lean, sharp-jawed man with haughty blue eyes and hair the color of golden wheat. He told us that the penalty under law for the crime of piracy was crucifixion. We would be tied to our crosses, whipped with rods, and made to suffer our wounds all night. Come morning, each man would be stabbed in the throat with a short sword—which he held up for all to see. The subsequent beheading and display of our severed heads would be of no concern at that point. He explained that the punishment would be carried out quickly, but that under law, he had no choice in the matter, or the method.

"By nightfall all of my shipmates, including the Egyptian, had been beaten bloody and fixed to their crosses, which were stood up in holes dug deep into the sand. The commander interceded for my life, if only to use me as a serving boy for the troops' dinner that night. So while my shipmates moaned and twisted on their crosses, I served up flat bread and salt fish by the wind-whipped blaze of our galley, which had been pulled ashore and set afire.

"That night, wrapped in the commander's cloak, I tried to sleep on the sand. But the agonies of my mates kept me awake. I saw them in the shifting light of the bonfire. My Egyptian had been set toward the front. His body was crisscrossed with bloody welts. He was still conscious, and when he saw that I'd been spared, he cried out for me.

"Hearing his cries, the commander took me aside and said, 'Is that man your lover?'

"'Yes, Lord.'

"'Then go to him.'

"I wasn't allowed to bring water because it would prolong life and suffering. For the same reason the Egyptian forbade me to tear off part of my tunic and try to wipe his wounds. He wanted death to come quickly now. So I sat at the base of the crucifix, which was all he asked. Once I was there he didn't complain about his suffering. So I sat. The wind died down, and the tide wash gradually worked its effect on me. The world was as cold as the sea, or as warm. Repetition was the only reality.

"Gradually the fire from our galley reduced to embers, and on the back of my neck I felt the occasional drops of warm blood dripping from the Egyptian's feet. The commander had given me a few swallows of wine, and this allowed me to sleep. I awoke with his cloak around me. My Egyptian was barely breathing.

"In the morning the Marines cut down the bodies and did the stabbing. Their method was to hold the flat of the sword blade up against chin before thrusting. This ensured the quickest death, and I concede it was done efficiently, and without taunting or mockery. Long stakes were then driven along the beach above the tide line, and the dead were beheaded with large-bladed axes. Each man's crucifix served as a chopping block. I carried the gore-smeared timbers back to the loading skiffs, watching my shipmates' blood pool on the warming sand.

"When the heads were impaled on the stakes, we disembarked. The commander placed me on his flagship, and while I held onto the stern rail of the swift-pulling galley, he surreptitiously caressed my arm. The scene on land shrank, the fence of heads—wind blowing their hair every which way—blended into the background of rock and sand, and the bodies, strewn around at random, drew crowds of gulls and vultures. I watched until distance put the beach out of sight.

"I'm not ashamed of my past. Life on ship taught me how to manipulate men. For us, the sting of immediate pleasure, the need for release, wants also a sense of triumph: *yes, you're the biggest, the sweetest! Yes, yours feels better than his!* What clowns and fools we are!

"The commander brought me home and kept me first as his instrument of pleasure. His own father had been a prince in southern Gaul, captured in a battle against Marius, and later given his freedom for good service. Now he had a wife of your upper classes, but still needed this affirmation, this sense of triumph. And so I gave it to him. I told him he meant everything to me. My complete surrender overpowered him, and he began to reciprocate. There were times when the tables were turned, when I wanted the affirmation, and my lover gladly complied.

"He taught me how to read and write, and set me free when he became a grandfather. The drive was gone and he knew it, not the drive for release, for he still had that, but that deeper desire for my complete submission was no longer important. So he released me with gold in my pocket. I travelled briefly through your city, then went back home and outfitted a ship and a crew of men.

"By then your people were too busy killing each other, and no other nation would stand against us. So we ruled the seas from Spain to Asia. Then our king, Mithridates, emboldened by your weakness, made a pact with Sertorius the one-eyed Spaniard. We were to become his navy.

Sertorius spoke to us on the deck of a flagship and was followed up the gangplank by a white fawn with flower garlands around its neck. Everyone said the fawn gave Sertorius godlike powers, and that he could never lose a battle.

"Sertorius promised to restore the republic to virtue, return its boundaries to the boot-shaped peninsula, and give political rights to all. We Cilicians would be ruled by Mithridates once more, and Greece would be ours as well. So we gave him our ships, and while helping him invade the islands off Spain, my galley was lost in a storm near Ibiza. I clung to a broken spar, and after being rescued, signed on as a slinger with a troop of Libyans.

"I'd never marched with an army before, and it was hard going for a short-legged man. An army is like a moving city. You sleep in a camp with orderly rows of streets and tents. Then you move out and the city becomes a river, flowing from one horizon to the next, meandering in open country, choked and turbulent in the narrow passes, disappearing in the woods and flowing deep in the valleys. You have supply trains and quartermasters. You have dust and honking mules and the endless double file of strong-legged infantry with field packs slung over their shoulders. Marching between them with their oak staffs are the iron-hard centurions, who keep discipline. These men are the high priests of battle, feared by the rank and file even more than the enemy.

"And so I fought at the River Sucro, after Sulla sent Pompey to crush Sertorius. Pompey charged straight into our volleys of missiles. After withstanding those stones which should have killed him, he shook himself like a dog coming out of the water, buckled his helmet, then came straight at me with his spear levelled, fixing me with a cold, murderous look. He'd picked me out as the man who cried out against him and whose stone almost brought him down.

"He charged straight, shouting *Eja! Eja! Alala!*—your battle cry, and a fearsome thing to hear, especially when the ranks of legionaries took it up.

"Luckily that dart struck him in the fleshy thigh muscle above the knee, so the wound was serious, but not killing. He fell from his horse before he could reach me. His men carried him off, but our Libyan skirmishers began such fighting over his horse and trappings that our line began to buckle. I retreated back to the camp just as Sertorius came up and routed Pompey's cavalry.

"But such is the confusion of battle that I found our camp overrun with enemy. They were killing everyone in sight. I threw off my sling and sidearm and crawled under a wagon, from which they pulled me out by both legs.

"While trying to convince them I was an officer's valet and not a soldier, Pompey came up on a horse, and seeing me, slid down and came over.

"I was immediately put on my knees, and my head bent down, forbidden to look upon the great man. But I saw the bandage on his thigh where the dart had struck.

"Pompey grabbed my hair and lifted my head up.

"He said, 'This one spoke my name.' His wide, dark eyes took me in, but his face was completely blank. This was a man of stone. He released me and I was put in the prisoner train as part of his personal baggage. They marched me into Italy and then to his gladiator school at Capua.

"Of course I was trained. They didn't just throw me into the arena in a Samnite's getup. They fed me well, built up my body, pampered me with physicians, trainers, and men who could massage so much fatigue from your muscles it felt as if your soul had flown—but only until the fear crept back in.

"I was a clown at first, amusing the crowd with mock fights. My usual opponent was a monkey in a legionary costume, trained to throw a javelin and close with the short sword. After a little of this so-called combat the monkey—at my command—would kneel and beg for mercy, and I would turn to the crowd for a verdict. This was invariably to let him live. At my command the poor beast would drop his weapons and jump into my arms, and I would hold him like a baby and pretend to cry in remorse as I kissed him. The crowd loved me for it.

"That was the easy part. Later I fought in real contests, first in the smaller arenas, then on to Paestum, Pompeii, the city itself. *Non Missio* was our school motto. We guaranteed our death. 'Don't show fear,' we told each other, 'fight hard. . . . 'Let's die well, for our own dignity.'

"And so you die well. This is your propaganda, and we fell for it. Don't raise your finger for mercy, but calmly remove your helmet and expose your neck to the killing thrust, and hope that it's fast. This was yet another world, another reality.

"But I wanted *not* to die well. I wanted to die like a coward to spite them, to make them angry, to take away their satisfaction, to make them sick with themselves. But I feared it, I feared the degradation of slow death.

"Thus I played into your hands.

"As a member of Pompey's team, I took part in the games he sponsored to win over the mob. And I've seen the spectacles, leopards pulling racing chariots, bulls fighting bears, pickpockets thrown to the beasts, lions pitted against black tribesmen plucked from the edges of the earth, with the arena decorated with false jungle foliage.

"Pompey never forgot my face, and one day he came to Capua to find me. So many of the wealthy tour the schools, led by the director through the training pits. It was a hot day and I was practicing sword work on a dummy. Although my eyes were blurred with sweat I immediately sensed the aura of a great man, the mood of awe created in the air about him. You know great men when you see them. Even our arrogant director was humbled, a man so high and mighty that he never hesitated to beat us with his fists for making mistakes. Oh, how I love your people!

"I'll admit that I cringed under the stare of those blank, dark eyes. Here was a man surely born with an empty spot in his soul, an oblivion to feeling that kept him apart from other men.

"Pointing me out to the director, Pompey said, 'This is the one.' Then he passed on to another part of the school. I heard the director say the words 'something special,' to a further remark Pompey made. For weeks after that I slept badly, believing the 'something special' would be Pompey's revenge on me.

"But to those who attend the games, my fate was ordinary. It's common for your people to explore everything to excess, including death. They particularly relish the deaths of the brave ones who mock fate by surrendering their hard-won freedom and returning to the arena for glory and money—the crowd deifies these men. Having lost their sense of personal valor, your people honor nothing more than heroism in others, victory against all odds. But heroism being rare in the arena, they feast on poor fare in greater amounts. Vicious butchery whips them into a frenzy, and they wallow in the false tragedy of prearranged death.

"Wounds and maiming such as mine are no more than the squeaks of a dying hare to those whose jaded appetite needs constant relief from the boredom of having nothing to do. For the politicians know that too much boredom will stimulate the brain to thought, even to political action. So your mob is pampered and feared, and barely notices anything less than sensational violence. A man with a puncture wound in his side, another with a severed limb, those who limp off with broken bones that never heal properly, these are mere table scraps. When boredom sets in at the games, they strangle a few slaves while waiting for the next contest.

"They trained me as a Samnite, short sword and square shield, like your legionaries use, and they would often match me against taller men as a way of showing how your method of fighting surpasses all others. So I faced Thracians with curved scimitars and small round bucklers, and I learned how to 'get inside' the *retiari*, with their long tridents and cunningly thrown nets. I was a dangerous swordsman not only because of my fast reflexes, but because I was left-handed, and this is a deadly anomaly.

"My fear that 'something special' was being cooked up was replaced by more immediate fears. I was fighting for my life, and killed my man each time, coming ever closer to the promise of freedom, which would come after fifty victories, or with luck, by some exemplary behavior before the Master of the Games.

"Then came the games in honor of Pompey's triumph for Spain and Libya. Pompey was loved as no other general, and this was a long-awaited day for your city. It began with drumming in the streets, then the parade horns joined in with stirring music. The procession was led by ranks of haughty legionaries in polished iron helmets, followed by lion-headed aquilifers holding their Eagles high, cohort and legion pennants rippling in the breeze. Then came the marching ranks of centurions with their oak staffs, cavalry from Gaul and Africa, long-haired men, men of all colors, people you've also enslaved or coerced to take your side, and the main attraction, carts of prisoners caged like animals, suffering the obscene taunting of the crowd, who throw rotten fruit or make foul gestures. These poor wretches will be marched into the Temple of Jupiter and have their throats slit in the ancient dungeon while Pompey prays to your god of gods.

"Then Jupiter himself—our Pompey—the Great Man's face daubed with red chalk. Solemn and terrible in his demeanor, he barely acknowledges the crowd and grips the rails of a chariot drawn by the sacred white horses, prancing, muscular beasts so hot-blooded that their flared nostrils seem to spout fire.

"Add to this spectacle the food served to the mob, meals for thousands on Mars Field, meat, wine, bread, fruits from all over the known world! And then the games, over one hundred contests to the death. Such days are feasts of blood as well!

"We marched in that parade behind a banner emblazoned with our school motto—*Non Missio*—and the crowd cheered us well. Later we waited in the arena's dark chambers while workers raked the sand on which we would sacrifice our lives. Above us we heard the steady footfalls of the crowd, the food hawkers crying out, the random outbursts of trumpets and drums as the musicians practiced, the slow but inexorable building of anticipation as the crowd filled the arena.

"While arming ourselves we heard the pre-contest ceremonies, consisting mostly of praise for Pompey's accomplishments, which included an accounting of how much gold and treasure he'd added to your state. We tried to ignore the wrestling matches and mock battles which followed, for they were the prelude to that all-too-familiar combination of trumpet notes signalling our contest. When these came we formed ranks and, simultaneous with fighters from the rival school, we marched into the arena's blinding light.

"There is nothing like that shock of emerging from quiet, cool darkness into the heat and light of an arena filled with a crowd hungry for blood, men and even your women, yes, women, screaming so frantically that their showers of spittle glinted in the sun. These were people so starved for the spectacle of death and maiming that we were almost crushed by their pressure. My knees buckled, and a few men in our ranks began to keen for their impending deaths.

"'*Be strong*,' we told each other. '*Be strong!*'

"Such was my state of mind that I forgot about that 'something special' Pompey might have cooked up for me. He was that day's Master of the Games, and I saw him from the corner of my eye—dressed in royal purple with a laurel crown buried in his thick hair.

We were already sweat-soaked when the trumpets blew for the inspection of arms. With great fanfare the game officials checked our weapons, running their thumbs along the cutting edges of our swords and the tips of our tridents. When this was announced satisfactory, more trumpet blasts. The mob's appetite was whetted now, and they began to cheer and call out to individual fighters.

"Next came the drawing of lots. This was my chance to warm up, to show off with knee bends, stretches, shadow swordplay. All the while I would glance at the fighters from the rival school and wonder which one would be my opponent.

"Small men like myself always fight first. I'd drawn an opponent a head taller, well built, and outfitted as a Thracian. His left arm, like mine, was encased in padded leather. No sooner had the trumpet blown for combat when I threw myself at him, fighting with all my fury, not caring whether I spent myself, pushing my large, heavier shield on him like a wall. I knocked him over by the abandon of my surprise attack.

"I'd pricked the crowd into wildness because death was to be delivered so quickly. But some cried out that I hadn't given the man a chance. This group won Pompey over, and he signalled for the fight to stop and begin again.

"So, both of us out of breath, we saluted him and readied ourselves. My opponent was blue-eyed, with a straight, narrow nose and full lips. The few words he'd spoken during our encounter were incomprehensible to me. Now we fell on each other with equal force. He pounded my shield with his sword, and each blow drove into the laminated wood. I realized that before long he'd hack my protection to slivers.

"Then I counterattacked, using my short sword to cut and thrust, its point and double edge looking to suck at any open place, as though blood were water and my sword a thirsty animal. That was how I saw it and how they taught me, using a trick of my mind to bring something about. Twice I cut into his leather armpiece, twice he knocked my sword aside with his own longer one, all the while maintaining the pressure with his shield.

"So we attacked and counterattacked, taking turns, as these battles usually go. One man attacks until he can barely hold up his weapon, the other defends and rests. I don't know how many times we did this, because when you fight there's an incredible focus. Yet images seep in. Later I remembered the red capes of the grandstand guards, the helmets and feathered plumes, the gold necklace around a woman's neck, all distinguished from the mass of humanity, fifty thousand people screaming for my blood.

"I then used an old trick. On the Gaul's next attack I crouched down, came up under his scimitar with my shield rim, and drove my sword up into his armpit, just above the place where the leather sleeve ends. I struck a junction of muscle and artery, for his arm suddenly became immobile, suspended in the air like a ship's boom. Blood gushed from his armpit with the regularity of a beating heart. His weapon fell to the sand and I kicked it away.

"I rammed him again with my shield, this time pushing him to the wall where the squealing crowd packed itself tighter to get a look. Now, in a change of heart, they were begging me to finish him off.

"He was praying in his own tongue then, for there was a blank look in his eye and his lip movements had the rhythm of a recitation. He spoke as he bled, in rhythmic spurts. Then he lifted the buckler over his face, and when it came away I saw that he'd removed his helmet, exposing his neck to the killing blow—which the rules demanded. He wore a torc around his neck; he had a spear of quicklime on his hair—something men of the north do when they go to war. He looked at me, then his eyes went blank. Death had entered his room.

"Later, days later, when I looked through my infirmary window at the stars, the white sparks of souls, I thought of the vanquished and felt sorry for them. But at that moment there was time only for work, and I knew how to make it fast and get away from the crowd. But when I looked at Pompey for approval, his thumb was up.

"His verdict spread through the stadium, and the crowd now began to hiss at me, crying that my victory was unfair. Pompey had swayed them. The Gaul was carried out, alive. I saluted the crowd, then Pompey himself, who barely acknowledged it. Then it struck me. This was it! This was all! This deprivation of victory was the 'something special' he'd spoken of. I couldn't wait for my weak legs to carry me to the exit gate. The crowd grew quiet, then broke into an anticipatory buzz, which I assumed was related to the next contest. But I was wrong. The exit was locked, and behind it, the director barked, 'Leave your weapons and go back. Pompey has something special for you.'

"So there it was. I heard stomping feet, peals of laughter, then a roar that travelled around the arena like an ocean wave. The crowd was crying out, 'Serves you right!" One man tried to wiggle down through the barriers to get at me but the guardsmen caught his feet and pulled him back. I looked around, seeing everything but what I was supposed to see. I thought of the wild beasts let loose in the arena, at first curious and puzzled by the raucous crowd, not yet seeing the mechanism of their doom. I headed for Pompey.

"He was facing me with his hands on his hips, and perhaps for the first time—the distance was great so I couldn't be sure—there was a spark in his eye, a glint of humor. He beckoned me closer and I came forward.

"The crowd stood up, cheering for Pompey, who raised one hand. They sat down immediately. Silence fell over all. I heard the breeze. I heard people coughing. Pompey motioned me closer, then called down to me.

"'Do you remember when we met? You hit me with a stone at Sucro. But you couldn't knock me down!'

"He raised both arms triumphantly, and the mob rose to its feet, screaming, stomping, calling Pompey's name in unison. Still, at that point, I thought this public humiliation was the extent of Pompey's revenge. After all, what had I done but my duty in battle?

"But later, again during those long infirmary days, I thought of something else, and conceded that even in the heat of battle, Pompey saw me as a particular threat. I'd called out to him in his own tongue, knowing that a Latin voice coming from a crowd of Libyans would get his attention. For a non-Roman to presume not only to call his name, but to call it in his own language, was to deliver an ultimate insult. This was why Pompey could remember me from the tens of thousands who wanted to kill him that day.

"A trumpet blew, and I turned to see a fighter coming toward me, a bright orange feather atop his helmet. He could have been my twin for he was small, dark, and hairy as a monkey. He advanced on me confidently, hefting a dagger in his right hand and a short sword in his left. Pompey had found my equal.

"I was given a new sword and a dagger, exactly like his. We saluted, then engaged, sword to sword and dagger to dagger, a game of cut, thrust, and dodge. Before long we were nicked all over, and the sharp weapons had mangled the protective leather on our arms. I'd cut him just below one eye and blood ran down over his mouth, so that he sucked blood when he inhaled, and sprayed it when he breathed out.

"We broke for a moment, breathing heavily. Our fatigue was such that we desperately needed to lower our arms to rest, yet knew that when one's guard is down, an attack follows. I was too tired even to taunt this opponent, who, so far, hadn't spoken one word, thus giving me no sign of his identity. During this brief moment I took a better look at what I could see of his face. He was beetle-browed, and his deep-set eyes were in shadow. It was impossible to know where he was looking. He gestured toward my dagger arm, which by reflex I used as a shield. It leaked a steady flow of blood onto the sand.

"The crowd, so much against me when I fought the Gaul, was now hushed at the skill of our combat. To a degree I'd redeemed myself, and maybe—it pains me to admit this—they would favor me again. So there we were, our shadows fixed on the sand, where one of us had stepped in a small puddle of blood—leaving a red sandal print. Was it his or mine?

"That look to the sand, that tiny speculation about whose footprint it might be, was my undoing. I awoke to his cut. The sound came first, like the swish of a dart. Then the blunt 'knock'—like a log being split for firewood.

"Despite all this, I thought I'd eluded the blow, and that the collective gasp of the crowd acknowledged my deft maneuver. But then, raising my dagger hand, I saw the stump spurting blood. But where was my right hand? So powerful is the mind that my first thought was of some defect in my vision, or even some elaborate trick. But with the first surge of pain came the reality, then the panic. Death was breathing in my ear, and Pompey would have his way.

"Holding the arm aloft to slow the blood loss, I attacked recklessly, willing to pay the price of my wounds, willing to die fighting rather than admit defeat and grant Pompey control over my life.

"These moments, as brief as the flap of a sparrow's wings, were filled with images of my life. The night before, at the dinner, when we gladiators took public supper with spectators drawn by lot, I had spoken with a man who lived for the *munis*, for the spectacle. He knew the names of gladiators from generations past, their statistics, whether they fought as Thracian, Samnite, or Net Man, how many they killed, whether they were wounded, how they were killed, whether gladiators were becoming better with time, and all the other silly considerations which occupy these worshippers of sport.

"This was a seedy, unshaven man with a wild look in his eye, who spoke as if these fighters were members of his family, who spoke as if he knew their motives and desires: *This one wants to retire in Campania, that one wants to start his own school.* With no life of his own, the man knew as much about me as I knew about myself, knew my past as a Cilician pirate, even as a slinger for Sertorius—his secret hero.

"So there my life reeled before me, the docks of Miletus, the bloody welts on my Egyptian's body, Sertorius' white fawn, the blooded horses pulling Pompey's chariot, their nostrils spouting fire. Simultaneous with these images, I saw my right hand lying on the sand, clutching and unclutching the dagger in its last pulsations. I died to that last sight, and briefly surrendered, satisfied to see the death's black curtain drop over my eyes as the crowd noise faded to silence. As I fell to the sand my eyes captured the gold and purple trim on a toga, a limp pennant, and finally, before he faded to black, Pompey on his feet, waving to me in farewell.

"I awoke with screams in my ears and visions of the shaded dead, convinced that I'd arrived in some underworld and joined the collective swoon, grouped with lives cut short before their time. I blacked out again, but my next awakening was quiet. From my bed the full moon looked like a luminous buckler embossed with maps of cities. I could barely move. My right arm was too weak to lift, and ended in a ball of blood-soaked bandages. On a nearby table sat a bowl of stinking liquid which the physician had been pouring down my throat to keep me alive.

"I learned that my opponent had been eager to deal the killing blow, but the crowd took my side, screaming for my life. Pompey, to his credit, set me free with a small stipend. I took a trader back to Miletus. The long sea journey gave me time to mull over my life, and to think of how to get even with your people, who were there at every turn to undo me."

~

Cutter and I are brothers in history, children of the same sea. This great lake touching so many civilizations—beyond which the world stretches into unimagined monstrosity—is the common stage of our lives.

Like Cutter, I was in the city for Pompey's triumph. I didn't parade in the great man's train as Cutter did, but watched it from a safe distance. Sulla had pardoned me, but a prohibition against death wouldn't preclude a good clubbing from Sulla's thugs, whose appetite for violence knew no bounds. My litter was ringed with bodyguards.

Pompey appeared as a blazing white jewel, the sun pouring its blessing on him. And he sent its gleaming rays out to all. He stood immobile in the chariot, more like a golden statue than a living creature, and the crowd—so typically frenzied in hatred for the city's enemies—loved him even more for his coldness. They supplied the heat. Old campaigners, their eyes wet with tears, raised their arms in salute, women bared their breasts for him to admire, vowing to suckle more warriors for our legions. Even this failed to turn the great man's head.

Envy kept me from the games later in the day, or I would have witnessed Cutter's mishap, and taken better measure of the man. But who could stomach another reiteration of Pompey's achievements—lands conquered, cities drained of their gold, prisoners taken, slaves added to our households, weapons and holy relics of other tribes now part of the national wealth. I was six years younger than the great man, yet such was my disposition that I lamented my birth. I'd come at the wrong time, when too many young men shared my ambitions.

The only balm for my soul was Servilia, whose litter stopped alongside mine just long enough for her to beckon me to follow her home. There I pulled the cotton shift down over her shoulders, and like a cat, rubbed my cheek against her back, travelling over the shoulder blades as though they were smooth hills, and kissing those beauty moles representing Italian cities: Mediolanum at the top of her spine, Rome near the rib cage, Brindusium at the coccyx.

"They told me you were home again," she said.

"Is it safe?"

"Probably. Sulla is dying."

Then her hands were all over me, under my garments, feeling my arms, chest, legs, feet, every part she could reach, almost frantic, like a merchant searching for lost goods.

"Everything's here," I said.

"For me?"

"Yes, for you."

"Do you love me?"

She held my eyes, looking for the truth. She liked this little play. Did I love her? Did I love those knife-blade lips, and even more, her way of understanding me?

"You think like a man, and that's why I love you."

"How is that?"

"You never ask the wrong questions."

"Which means?"

"You know that there is love, and love."

"No, there's love, and there's politics. We love each other for mutual strength. This is why you can love me and still have your marriage."

~

On the pier at Miletus the masts of traders sway with the tide, and stevedores unload goods from every city in our world, bending the gangplanks under the weight of ebony and ivory. Anyone disembarking from these ships must endure a gauntlet of sharks and pickpockets, crowds of starving boys, or clusters of surly, rotten-toothed men in pointed boots whose object is to steer the unsuspecting toward a nearby maze of buildings and narrow alleys containing nothing but taverns, brothels, and sites for attack.

This confluence of treachery makes Cutter nostalgic for his old life. We no sooner step off his flagship—to the governor's commissioner, who supervises the exchange—when he leaves me for a gang of boys who spend their time accosting sailors. He speaks to them in rapid, animated Cilician, and they're all ears, for as he did when young, they admire anyone who enriches himself with such apparent ease.

"I wanted to give them money," he says, returning to me. "Your money of course. But they wouldn't take it. Instead they offer me some interesting pleasures in another part of the city."

"They're more sophisticated than you were at that age."

His brow furrows. "How do you mean, Lord?"

"They were investing in your trust."

"I know that trick," Cutter says.

"I'm not so sure you do."

"Why do you say that?"

"Because I'm playing it on you too."

"How is that, Lord?"

I gesture toward the men loading sacks of gold coins onto the flagship.

"My part of our bargain is carried out. Wouldn't you say that you trust me?"

"To the hilt, Lord."

"Then my point is made."

Now we hear the graceful notes of a flute and a soft, drumming beat. The door of a brothel swings open and some musicians file out, followed by several prostitutes. Dressed in gay silks and brass platelets, with head ornaments made from the mesh of delicately woven chains, the women stride boldly in our direction, gyrating their hips and calling merrily to the sailors and passers by. They cross the pier and ascend the gangplank onto Cutter's galley. Some of the men take them below decks immediately.

The musicians play on board the galley while the joyful shrieks of the women emerge from below decks. "Mere boys," says Cutter derisively, "Boys with no patience. But we will feast tonight, Lord, on partridge and young lambs, on great planks of flat bread and nothing but the best wine,

Falernian! Grown in the province where you hid from Sulla, and stolen from your own traders!"

As the last of the bags full of coin are loaded, some of the pirates cry out, "Goodbye, Lord, and thank you for making us rich!" Others bow low or fold their hands in signs of mock prayer. "Pardon us, Lord. We were only following orders! Pardon us, *Imperator*!" Goras, at the tiller, looks at me and shrugs his shoulders to make me understand that he's not part of it.

Cutter says, "Disregard the men, and forget the money. I've given you the story of my life in exchange, with the hope it will do some good. We're on the same side anyway, Lord, against the Sullans, and for Sertorius! He's a Popular, like you, to be sure. Now you know me and where I've been. You carry, so to speak, part of my spirit."

He brings his left fist to his heart to emphasize the point. Then a looped rope swings over from the galley. He grasps it with one hand, then turns to me, tapping the ram's head on the clasp holding my cloak.

"You're not thinking about coming after me, are you?"

"Why would I do that?"

"Smart boy," he says, hugging the rope. Then placing one foot in the loop, he swings away and aboard, his baggy pantaloons billowing in the breeze.

The pirates hoist their purple-trimmed sails, and under wind power the galley slips deftly around the other ships in the harbor. Once in open water its silver-tipped oars extend from port and starboard like arms, and begin their unified dipping and pulling to the rhythm-keeper's drum. The men on deck call and wave to me, some of them holding up the gold sacks. I don't return their goodbyes. Cutter stands on the stern deck and calls out something I can't understand, but the tone is clear—he's pleased with himself.

The galley shrinks in the distance, and with its diminution, my ascendance. Curio appears at my side, scratching his bristly beard. I feel his gaze.

"Are you ready, Lord?"

"You have the men?"

"Assorted wharf rats, local militia, and the retired military in command."

"Are they hungry?"

"Starving."

"Let's wait until he's out of sight."

The fop's clothing worn for the pirates has been shed like a player's mask. Now, fitted out in leather and bronze, I stride the deck of a state war galley, inspecting my ranks of marines.

Not one hour out of Miletus the gods see fit to test me by blowing great storm clouds across the sky, and no sooner do the first whitecaps appear when my three ship captains, making gestures toward the western sky, where lightning-veined clouds loom before us, signal to turn back and fight another day. Not wanting to lose our advantage, I refuse the request and order them to follow into the whistling squalls which sweep the sky of our guiding stars. The wind digs up swells higher than the ships' prows, so that we're thrust into a world of towering, angry waves. We take them head-on. The swells are mountains whose peaks our diminutive warship climbs and tops. Then we descend, crashing into the iron-hard troughs, the sea flooding our deck. A prolonged thunderbolt lights a world in which sea and sky desire to mate, the air speckled with flying gobs of foam jetting into the vault and there disintegrating. Then total blackness again, and every man gropes for a hold on something, a rail, the mast, or any of the ropes tied on the deck. The next thunderbolt lights the world briefly. Three ships are gone, sunk or out of sight, and disordered ranks of sick and frightened men now hold on for their lives.

The gods now cry, "You've yet to see our power!" They hurl bolt after bolt. Thunder crashes like mountains split asunder, or great oaks instantly rent, and the men point to the teetering masts of our sister ships visible behind the walls of water, and whether the ships are sunk or afloat we can't tell. The light is eerie but bright, flickering as the bolts make their way across great distances of sky like pathways of gold.

At the foredeck rail, Curio stands with his hair hanging down in wet strands, arms upraised to the storm. He cries out, "More, you winds! More, you thunderbolts! Give us more! Give us all your rage!"

As if his words were a perverse command, the storm soon subsides. Here is the power of the gods. The thundering gale reduces to a whistle, then a sweet breeze. The walls of angry waves lower to calmer swells, and we enter placid seas with cool, slow-moving air. The stars are a great smear of white, and the northern constellations glow like pearls.

I join Curio on the foredeck, and he stretches out his hand as if to present this new world to me. Our sister ships now appear beside us, all three, regrouping, their oars reaching into the water, and we move like many-armed creatures. Curio orders lamps to be lit, and the decks of the ships appear like distinct, luminous worlds. We glow with long walls of brass-rimmed shields and stacked plate armor, javelins bristling along the rails. The sky illuminates Scorpions with piles of stones ready to throw, and boarding ramps hoisted high, each with a massive steel spike to make us fast to an enemy deck. From amid each galley the grinding wheels turn, and as the men line up to sharpen their weapons, the showers of sparks create a second glow on each deck. Then the lamps are extinguished and we become four black shapes, giant water beetles skimming the still sea, no sound but dipping oars and cutting prows hissing like snakes.

The dawn of quiet red embers bursts into a curtain of liquid fire, and behind this wall of blinding light Apollo mounts his car and takes the reins. His horses pull the great sphere high above the Asian forests to whisk away the world's black garments. The sea is illumined like a great jewel, and Cutter's island is born, a tiny iridescent kingdom in a glasslike sea, the sun's hand flat on its rocky hills and rust-colored cliffs.

~

Of course he knew all along that I'd return in force. And were it not for the storm we would have surprised him on land, perhaps asleep. He didn't think my force would be organized so soon, and luck would have it that when we neared the harbor mouth, all of Cutter's fleet—four ships in single file, decks laden with their collected booty—were heading for the open sea.

There was no choice but to engage them in the harbor, so leaving two ships to prevent their escape, we attack with our remaining two, and our Scorpions' stones rip through their sails crash to the decks, where they shatter the racks of amphorae the pirates hoped to salvage.

Our two ships having reached the end of Cutter's line, we circle in opposite directions, continuing our missile barrage. Coming up on Cutter's flagship from both sides, we drop our ramps. But while the contingent of marines on our partner ship has no difficulty boarding, our own ramp hangs up in the trireme's rigging. I climb the ramp with several men and hack the rigging until the ropes give way and our weight brings us crashing to the deck.

Outnumbered, and taken by surprise, the pirates make for the rails, slipping on the oil, wine, and fish paste from the amphorae they'd loaded on board. A few lucky ones manage to slither overboard and swim for shore. Those remaining on deck cover their heads with their hands and beg for their lives. Many of these point below, where Cutter is found hiding in a compartment containing the ransom.

They bring him topside and he sits cross-legged on the deck, gripping the ram's head with his good hand as if keeping it warm. His men file past him in leg irons and he turns his head to follow each one, muttering their names. When one of them spits on his head he rubs his scalp and smiles.

"Are you satisfied now?" I ask.

The words move him to lift his gaze, but not all the way. I walk around him, as he did to me so many times. He looks up, shrugs, and holds out an empty hand.

"What are you now?" I ask.

"Nothing, Lord."

"And what do you think of me?"

"The better man, Lord, clearly the better man."

"You're thinking to bribe your way out of this, aren't you."

"No, Lord, I'm done. I surrender."

"You're trying to do the same thing now, aren't you?"

"And what is that, Lord?"

"Invest in my trust."

He looks away, through the ship's rail to the settlement on shore where the last of his men are being rounded up. I remind him that playing the same game twice never works.

~

Forty days ago I would have been castrated and sold to some satrap with a penchant for western boys. But now, having recovered the ransom and returned it to the money lenders, having paid the men with the pirates' treasure, and with a profit for myself, fortune, once repelled by the odor of my breath, now kisses me with open mouth.

There being no prison in Miletus, I deliver Cutter and his men to the nearby city of Pergamum. Here, below the towering acropolis lies the prison, a rough stone building without windows, an oven to bake its inmates. I supervise the jailing, making sure that the men remain shackled in their cells. Then I climb to the home of the gods.

The Pergamum Acropolis rises from the valley in a nearly sheer wall so towering that it evokes awe and fear. The citadel itself is higher than that of Athens. The temples are built of blue-and-ochre-dyed marble. Even from below, their gilded reliefs and edge-work blind the eye. The climb is long and steep, and every so often I stop to rest, looking west to the point where sea and sky are one, then down to the river valley, where the tree tops are tiny tufts of green. My destination is the Altar of Zeus, which lies on a plateau just below the summit.

The Altar is an immense marble frieze that could be the wall of a small city. Its top supports the allotted spaces for sacrifice and fire. The carved marble on the sides depicts the revolt of the giants against the Olympian gods, the former oozing from the earth as half-man, half-snake, to hurl boulders and burning oak trees at the sky. The gods attack with the help of a mortal bowman—Hercules—and the frieze presents the individual battles. Here are Zeus and Hercules killing Porphyrion with thunderbolt and arrow; Apollo and Hercules standing triumphantly over the dying Ephialtes who clutches the arrows in each of his eyes, Apollo's in one and Hercules' in the other. Ephialtes' face twists in pain as blood spurts from his eye sockets. Next we see Athena crushing Encyclades with the island of Sicily, then flaying Pallas and using his skin for a shield. Nowhere, not in the poetry of any nation, do we see the gods in such fury. An inscription over the frieze tells us that the battle against the giants commemorates the victory of King Attalos over the marauding Gauls more than one hundred years ago, those same Gauls who sacked our city in the time of Servilia's great-grandmother.

At this great height the wind's bleak, isolated whistle reminds one that the gods reside precisely in those places hostile to man. All the more stirring is this reach for the divine. I'm in the actual presence of the gods, and this carved marble panorama of their terrible ferocity overwhelms me to dizziness. I sit on the nearest steps, studying the altar figures in every aspect. To the west, to home, I look out to the glistening Ciacus River and the fertile valley with its orderly allotment of fruit and olive groves, and great smears of green wheat fields. Several worshippers come up the steps, all Greeks, merchants and ship owners, dignified, self-contained men who operate the machines of world commerce. Here they seek divine auguries, necessary in these days when savages control the seas and our state is threatened from all sides.

I'm with the gods, not the giants, and thus I have no choice. Cutter and his men must know this.

I eavesdrop on the Greeks speaking their sensuous language, then make my way higher up to the treasury near the Temple of Athena. A young priest with a spotless tunic takes my coins and gestures that the place is mine. I walk to the outer walls of the citadel and look down. Below me lies the upper town market with its braying animals and aggressive hawkers whose singsong weaves into the liquid notes of a flute. The music and this place joins man and god. And when I descend from these whistling heights to the world of work and pain, of choice and obligation, the world in which one must keep his promises or be nothing, I'll need to remember this: that the gods don't live in one place and man in another. In some form, the gods are within the thinking man, and the sense of justice one espouses must be divine-based. To sentence scores of men—exactly eighty-eight, a number with its own justice—to the ultimate punishment, is a promise that must be kept, and the only future for Cutter and his men is a half-life in the underworld. Killing men, I create souls, and nothing is taken from the balance of the earth. This is one rationale. The other is that I'm part of this world, having been born into a state of war—the Sullans oozing from the earth like rebellious giants—and what would be said of me if I denied my station, allowed Cutter and his crew to bribe their way out of the prison below and continue their former lives? I must be Caesar, for in this world, rebellion is constant.

I must be, but am I? In thinking moments the parts that I play peel from my mind like the layers of an onion: the poet, the man of taste, the personification of Roman Law, the outraged, the executioner. In my core I could be satisfied as a temple priest living on the money from supplicants . . . anywhere but in Rome, that city more ravaged than Sulla's visage. Achievement, divine lineage, ambition, whether I'll survive the Sullans, whether Servilia knows my future, she with the lips like knives, the nipples as red as blood, she who swims with me over the warm seas of lovemaking, all this is the purple cloth of vanity concealing the chains in which I'm shackled.

~

Just south of Miletus lies a small beach where the coarse, rust-colored sand filters the sea waves. The shoreline is steep here, and a string of small islands forms a natural harbor mole. The shipping lane runs between the shore and the islands, and there are no breakers. The sea rises and falls in foamy swells as the tide works in and out. Every ship entering Miletus from the west must pass this way. This is our place of justice.

Squads of police lead the prisoners here, their legs shackled, each man's arms lashed to the crossbeam of his own crucifix. Other workers unload the timber posts from carts and plant them along the beach. This quiet, tide-lapping place soon becomes a small city, a place of curses and cries. Mounted, I ride up and down on the hard sand near the water, setting distances. I want the crosses planted far apart and close to the surf so the pirates' can be seen by passing ships. Cutter will be in the center, and forward of the rest.

I order him brought before me, telling the guards to treat him gently. He trudges and half-stumbles over the sand, taking small steps under the restraints of his chains and the weight of his beam. He stops just short of my horse, his lowered head even with my foot. His ram's head stump was taken away at the prison, and the end of his severed arm is discolored and bulbous.

"Can you look at me?"

"No, Lord."

"I'm not surprised. You made a fatal judgment."

"I didn't think you'd return so soon."

"What did you think?"

"It doesn't matter now."

Now he turns up to me, forcing a smile his lips will not permit. They tremble. He looks past me and upwards, following a white sea bird gliding across the sky.

"Luck for you," he says.

I follow his gaze. The bird is a swan, with an orange beak and black face. Its flight is slow and graceful. I look in its eye, the gull's blue eye of forty days ago.

"Now consider the price," I say, gesturing along the beach as men with crossbeams on their shoulders are hoisted onto the timber posts. Many scream as their feet are nailed into place. "Look at the misery you've created for those who served you. Look what you've forced me to do!"

"Forced you, Lord?"

"After you slaughtered Secondini and his crew, after you destroyed his ship and cargo, do you think I have a choice?"

"But I'm a war prisoner, not a criminal. And I could have killed you too."

"Death would come either way."

"But not like this, not whipped with rods and made to suffer all night."

"You know the punishment because you've seen it. Our laws are ancient and consistent. Pirates are whipped before hanging."

"And consideration for the mercy shown to you?"

"I've given the order to forego the whipping, for all of you. This is in exchange for the mercy you've shown to me and my staff."

This time his lips are steady when he smiles. "This only means we'll die more slowly, of thirst and hunger, of tiny wounds in our feet which won't bleed fast enough. We'll welcome the pecking of carrion birds."

"You won't die slowly."

"And why is that, Lord?"

"Because I've arranged that as well."

He gives me a conspiratorial look, then shakes his head as if to get rid of some pain.

When I don't elaborate, he says, "No matter. All is written, Lord, written down beforehand. So why should we thank you for this illusive mercy? My end is old news. The fisherman who lived on the island and sucked the wisdom of the sea into his body, he saw my fate, and had he met you, would have seen yours. No man is forced, Lord, to punishment or mercy, especially one like yourself. Save the political gestures for the senate of your great city, and do your work here. I'm ready for whatever you measure out. I'm ready for the curtain to fall."

"It's impossible . . ." I begin.

"For what?"

"For an equal exchange between us. Nothing I do will suffice."

"Except to die."

I salute him as the soldiers hoist his crosspiece, then nail his feet, one spike in each. He doesn't cry out when the blood flows. I leave him and canter down the line. The process is in full swing now. Eighty-eight posts are set, the tools distributed. Soldiers lead each man to his destination. Some need to be dragged over the sand. I pass those with whom I've spent my time on the island, those who mocked, those who insulted, those who threw the javelin and ran against me in the games. A few avert my gaze, others pray for mercy, clasping their hands and crying out to me. They've become beggars for their lives, cowering, unshaven, and stinking from prison, where they were stripped of their clothing and given rough, tattered garments to wear. *Mercy, Lord.* They all say it, the dart men who killed Secondini's crew mutilated their bodies for a few bits of gold, the insolent ones who called me *Imperator* or *faggot*, those who held up the money sacks and gestured with mock obeisance. *Mercy, Lord, I had nothing to do with it.*

I hear the cries of Goras and see him in the front row, distinguished by his great belly.

"Take me in your service, Lord. I'll serve you loyally."

"I know that."

"I always treated you with respect, Lord."

"And you liked my poetry."

His response is cut off by a spasm of pain, for his great weight pulls on the nails and opens his wounds even further. I order more ropes to hold him up and ease the pain, then say goodbye and turn away. When he cries out, "I thought you were my friend!"—I urge my horse to a more remote place.

This beach is an open temple of fate. Like angry bees, the soldiers in yellow armor and black capes wrestle the prisoners to the posts, mortise the crosspieces, set each man's feet into a wooden rest, and drive the nails to hold them fast. The air rings with the sound of hammers and the agonies of the guilty. I canter my horse along the tide line. Above the groans and cries my name flies in the air, as though the gods are speaking it. *Caesar! Caesar!* On the lips of men, in the lapping tide, my name bubbles up in the salty foam, the chant of two syllables, *CAE-SAR! CAE-SAR!* The tidal flow sings my destiny, rising, rising, foaming, yet steady and white like the swan. My name sails above the cries of the doomed. There's no way to tell them that I am doomed to this as they to death.

Cutter faces the sea, his head moving from side to side as if to deny this is happening to him. His feet drip blood.

"Is it better with the weight off your arms?" I ask.

"You test me, Lord, to the limit."

"Are you comfortable?"

"Oh yes, Lord, very comfortable."

I urge my horse closer and wave the nearby men out of earshot. For the first time now we are the same height. I stare at him until he brings his eyes from the sea and looks into mine.

"You want to say something, don't you, Lord?"

"A few last words, something between us."

"I have no regrets."

"I think you do."

"Are those your last words? For if they are, well and good."

"I have some other words."

"Lord?"

I pause, look out to sea for a moment. There is no swan, only a band of glittering sunlight. Turning back to Cutter I say, "My second poem, that you didn't have a chance to hear."

He looks to the sky for tolerance. "And must I suffer this now?"

"There's something in it for you."

"A lesson?"

"A return gift, my story for yours."

"I will hear it, Lord."

"Of course you will. This is a chance for you to mock me one last time."

He grits his teeth and forces the words. "Give me all of it, Lord, the whole poem. Hold nothing back."

"You're very kind. So here it is, from me to you, here and now. It will become part of what is written down, a song over this sand and these foaming waters."

"What is the poem called?"

"*My Father.*"

Old Anchises, standing on Ilium's wall,
his trembling hand arched over his eyes, the
better to see, observes the dust cloud of his
son's chariot. And like a wolf, the son hustles
across the plain of old Scamandros, moving to
buttress the line at its weakest point, hungry
to face the angry Argive heroes.

An old wolf himself, Anchises counts that
son like a miser counts coins, he with the
chariot the oldest minted, Aeneas, of
unalloyed gold, like the sun on his
shimmering helm, that coin pressed in
the days of honest kings, a weighty piece,
set with the image of a far-off city of hills, bathed
in sun and blessed by the God of Rivers.

This coin the old miser tucks into a
separate purse worn on a leather necklace
close to his heart. That young wolf, he knows,
sprang from Golden Venus, into whose womb
Anchises poured his seed when that Goddess came
to him on Mount Ida, and would, despite the
auguries of Cassandra, live to fight in other
lands, and his own divine seed begin a race of
Italians to surpass in greatness the tribes of
Greece and Troy combined.

And one of these, held captive near the
place of his first father, will soon play the
wolf again.

"So, what do you think?"

"A good poem, Lord."

"Do you understand the allusions?"

"I see what you mean, Lord."

"There's a lesson there."

"It's better than your last."

"Had you heard this poem on the island, things might have ended differently."

"I think not, Lord." He shrugs and I follow his gaze out to sea, where the trireme comes into view over the smooth, gold-tinted waters, its metal fittings aglow in the setting sun, the oarsmen pulling slowly, then lifting the oars as the anchors are thrown out. The ship's rails are hung with legionary shields, and flying from its mast, the ensigns and banners of our state, and the flag of my family gods.

"And what do you see now?"

"A good ship, Lord. I thought it was done for."

"It's been repaired, 'as a memorial' you might say."

"And may you use it well."

"It will serve."

"My work is in that ship, Lord."

"I will think of you."

We look at each other. His eyes begin to blink and the skin around them twitches. We look out to the sea. Some fishermen wading in the shallow water near the islands are pulling up nets laden with mullets. They work ignoring the activity on this beach.

"From the first moment I saw you . . ." Cutter begins, then stops.

"I understand, and perhaps for me too."

We watch as one of the fishermen leads a donkey into the surf and the fish are thrown into straw baskets slung over the animal's back.

Biting his lip against the pain, but speaking through it, Cutter says, "You would think that right now I envy those simple men who fish for a living and fear the gods and do as they're told. Their lives prepare them for death."

"Would you have it any other way? Would you like to have been one of them?"

"No, Lord."

He's still looking out to sea, as if he would fly there. His face is purple and swollen from being beaten at the prison.

"Are you ready?"

"No."

I place my hand on his shoulder and rest it there, not caring who sees me. Unlike what Pompey would have done, given the orders from afar, or Crassus the same, men whose justice would have been absolute.

"You are a poet, Lord."

I look at my hand on his shoulder. "This is the sign of a poet?"

"A true sign, that you see the connection between men."

"But you're not ready?"

"Some men are always ready for death, and perhaps I am, Who knows? The restless, unsatisfied hunger for life abandoned me when I lost my hand. Now I've drunk from the cup. I've seen the great men of our time. I've been swallowed by the sea and spat back up. I've been cheered and insulted by multitudes at a time, and I eventually devoted myself to the defeat of your state. It may yet come about."

I take my hand from his shoulder. The moment is over.

"Not in my time."

"Who knows, Lord. This victory of yours, this little show on the beach, will be written down for others. Everything is known, everything seen, if only by the gods, who have their way of speaking to man."

"You should have been a senator."

He looks out to sea, gesturing to the trireme rocking against its anchor ropes. "And you a pirate."

Up and down the line, all the pirates have been fixed to their crosses. Cutter tries to stare at me, but his eyelids begin to flutter. Now from the trireme one blast of a horn. Curio signals at the rail—one hand drawn across his neck. Then he holds out both hands, palms up.

"Your man wants it finished," says Cutter.

"He's always impatient."

The sun nears the horizon, and Cutter exhales from deep inside himself. "I should have killed you both." Still looking away, he says, "The night is ahead of us. Will you stay until the end, Lord?"

"Yes."

"Then I'll have the last word. Once the pain begins you'll see me die badly. All night long I'll insult you and your great city and call out the names of its victims. I've put them to memory, like you with your poem. I'll start with Secondini, that trader captain who eluded us so many times. And tomorrow, when my head is cut off, your men will have to throw it into the sea to quiet my voice. Even then, from the bottom of the sea my mouth will sing of the Romans I've beheaded, drowned, and robbed, mocking them because I've defied their law for so many years."

"That's not the way it will happen," I say, giving the signal to the men up and down the line. From my saddle pouch I take a length of soft, strong leather.

"What is this, Lord?"

"My promise."

"Of what?"

"A quick death." Gently saying, "Hold still now," I loop it around his neck, simultaneously urging my horse against the cross. When close enough for purchase, I pull the leather tight. Cutter's breath is choked off, and his face reddens. Up and down the line the soldiers follow my example and dispatch the pirates in the same way. The leather cuts into the beard on Cutter's neck and his face turns red, then blue. His eyes bulge out with shock, as his body strains against the ropes. I pull tighter, using all my strength now, unable to speak, but trying to tell him with my eyes that this is the most painless way to do my work. In the single nod of his head which precedes the empurplement of his face he seems to understand this. I pull until the life goes out of his eyes, and a look of outrage freezes behind the mask on his face.

~

This is my beginning, as certain as a beard's first growth, or the early pulsings of sexual desire. The work is done, although not to Curio's liking. He would whip them with rods and slit their throats after a night of suffering. "Think of poor Secondini and his men! Even more, think of your reputation." But if they in Rome criticize this as an excess of mercy, let them think back to Sulla and Marius, whose blood lust only fed on itself. So let us end it here, the price paid, my word kept, this little part of Our Sea made safe, for now, and the course of my life set.

Grouped in my wake and packed with Marines are Juncus's four warships. Our Sullan governor wanted to sell the pirates into slavery and pocket their treasury. He wasn't pleased that I'd taken matters—and money—into my own hands. To soothe his feelings I've agreed to do him a favor: contingents of Mithridates' army have crossed our borders not two days sail from here. With his force I plan to attack and give our governor some credit for protecting our borders.

The deck of Cutter's trireme sways under my feet, and I grip the rail to prevent the oar surge from pitching me into the sea. This galley powers through the swells, almost as if the sea were flat and calm. At each rise the beach near Miletus comes into view, tinted red from the setting sun and shrinking constantly. The crosses are still discernible, like children's play sticks in the sand. Cutter is forward of the rest, ready to receive the pack of vultures who settle on the sand and stride toward him like generals. I shudder to think of what language might pass between them. Soon sea mist covers all, and turns my attention forward.

The young man in bright clothing and hand-carved boots who fiercely defended his poetry, and who, in the midst of barbarity, insisted on the refinements of civilization, returned to uphold the law these dead men laughed at. Thus it will be written.

TO THE READER

While historians agree that Caesar kept his promise to return and crucify the pirates, the adventure isn't treated in detail. More is made of the young man's cunning and the first signs of a mercy remarkable for its author. In Caesar's last years this trait proved fatal.

After his adventure with the pirates and the brief military action against Mithridates' invasion force, Caesar would wait fifteen years for his next command. He went on to conquer all of France and parts of Germany, Spain, and Britain. He won the civil war against Pompey and the Optimates, and wrote of these achievements in a spare, elegant style which became the benchmark for Latin prose. The man associated with a million combat deaths and the man who cut off the right hands of whole tribes was the same who pardoned those peers who fought with Pompey. Among those spared was Marcus Brutus, Servilia's son, and a leader in the conspiracy. On the Ides of March his dagger would find its target in Caesar's groin. Yet even after the assassination, Caesar remained victorious in his prophecies: his death, as he had foretold, unleashed the dogs of civil war once again.

J. P.